Kissed by Cat

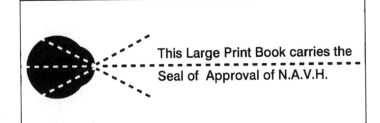

This Large Print Book carries the
Seal of Approval of N.A.V.H.

Kissed by Cat

Shirley Jump

Thorndike Press • Waterville, Maine

30272 7084

Published in 2005 by arrangement with Harlequin Books S.A.

Thorndike Press® Large Print Romance.

The tree indicium is a trademark of Thorndike Press.

The text of this Large Print edition is unabridged.
Other aspects of the book may vary from the original edition.

Set in 16 pt. Plantin by Carleen Stearns.

Printed in the United States on permanent paper.

Library of Congress Cataloging-in-Publication Data

Kawa-Jump, Shirley.
    Kissed by Cat / by Shirley Jump. — Large print ed.
      p. cm. — (Thorndike Press large print Thorndike
romance)
    Originally published: Silhouette, 2005.
    ISBN 0-7862-8140-5 (lg. print : hc : alk. paper)
    1. Large type books. I. Title. II. Thorndike Press large
print romance series.
PS3611.A87K57 2005
  813′.6—dc22   2005022110

To my daughter, whose love of cats provided the inspiration for this book as well as many of the details about how cats behave, walk and think. Someday, I promise, you'll be old enough and I'll let you read past the first chapter. I love you, honey, more than words can say.

As the Founder/CEO of NAVH, the only national health agency solely devoted to those who, although not totally blind, have an eye disease which could lead to serious visual impairment, I am pleased to recognize Thorndike Press★ as one of the leading publishers in the large print field.

Founded in 1954 in San Francisco to prepare large print textbooks for partially seeing children, NAVH became the pioneer and standard setting agency in the preparation of large type.

Today, those publishers who meet our standards carry the prestigious "Seal of Approval" indicating high quality large print. We are delighted that Thorndike Press is one of the publishers whose titles meet these standards. We are also pleased to recognize the significant contribution Thorndike Press is making in this important and growing field.

Lorraine H. Marchi, L.H.D.
Founder/CEO
NAVH

★ Thorndike Press encompasses the following imprints: Thorndike, Wheeler, Walker and Large Print Press.

From the journal of Hezabeth, the witch: Curse #581:

I had a perfectly good black cat, until Catherine Wyndham came along and set it free, like some do-gooder on an animal rescue mission. So I cursed her. Hee-hee-hee.

Yes, I did. I cursed her but good. If she loves animals so much, I told her, she could have a taste of life as one. I tossed my magic powder at her and in the language of the ancients said, "By day a woman, by night a cat. The curse can only be broken if you find a man who loves you as both."

That's never going to happen. No man in his right mind would love a woman like that. Especially not when he sees what happens to her when the sun goes down.

Hee-hee-hee. Sometimes, I'm too bad for my own good!

Chapter One

Being chased down Broward Street by an ugly, hungry Great Dane at one in the morning did not rank on the top ten of Catherine Wyndham's favorite ways to spend an evening. She'd much rather have been curled up in front of a fireplace with a fuzzy blanket, a saucer of warm milk and a freshly opened can of tuna.

The lumbering beast of a dog opened his jaws and lunged forward. Catherine scampered up someone's back porch, across the railing and into the next yard, leaving the dog barking at nothing but cold November air.

For the ten thousandth time in two hundred years, Catherine regretted ever tangling with that witch. She'd always had a bad habit of helping stray and mistreated animals. She'd picked the wrong black cat one day and had thus been cursed by Hezabeth the Witch to live a half life —

which was really no life at all.

Today, though, had been a good day, relatively speaking. Catherine turned the corner, quite pleased with her getaway.

She jerked to a stop. There it was. Their scent. She lowered her head to the ground, concentrating as she tracked. Her instincts perked up, telegraphing a warning signal, but she ignored it.

Five more seconds. I've almost —

And then she was being scooped up by a pair of strong, masculine hands. She shrieked and tried to twist away but the man held tight, depositing her into a small metal cage, with no more effort than he'd use to flick a whip.

She let out a second scream of protest. "I know, I know," he said in a soft, crooning voice. "Right now, you probably hate me, but believe me, it's for your own good."

She glared back, swatted at the bars. Futile gestures. He had the upper hand — not to mention bigger hands that could transport her anywhere he wanted her to go.

She hated that. Hated being eight inches tall and about as powerful as a gnat wrestling a gorilla.

He *did* have a kind face, at least. Better to be kidnapped by a prince than an ogre.

She'd been with both in the last two centuries. Handsome didn't always equal nice or bright, but it did provide a better view.

Ugly or cute, none of the men she'd met had been the knight in shining armor that could end the curse put in place by Hezabeth — her revenge against Catherine for setting the witch's cat free.

"You love animals so much, how about a taste of life like one?" the witch had cackled. Before Catherine could get away, Hezabeth had thrown some powder at her and muttered something in an ancient language. From that day forward, Lady Catherine Wyndham, heir to the Wyndham estates and fortune, daughter of the Earl and Countess of Wyndham, had ceased to exist. And, thanks to Hezabeth's addition of a catch-22 twist, Catherine had no hope of ever breaking the curse with some storybook ending.

It didn't matter. Finding Prince Charming wasn't at the top of her To Do list. Hadn't been in fifty-odd years. *If* he even existed, the chances of meeting him when she wasn't sporting whiskers were pretty slim.

In the half light of the car, she could see a day's worth of stubble on the man's chin, softening the hard edges of his jaw. Faint lines zigzagged down the left side of his face, disappearing beneath his collar.

Scars. From what? From who?

Her gaze skipped over the marks and connected with his eyes. Large, brown and almost . . . soft.

They looked at her with a kindness and compassion she'd rarely seen in two hundred and twenty-five years of life. She'd traveled the world, by land and by boat, before ending up in the United States and now, the Midwest. All those cities, all those people, and not one had seen her as much more than a waste of DNA. But now, in this small city in Indiana, a man with an almost empathetic gaze.

As if he understood.

Impossible. No one knew what she'd gone through. What a nightmare her life had been since Hezabeth had damned Catherine to an existence filled with pain and loneliness, one no sane person would find believable.

She shook herself. She must be due for a distemper shot. She was getting maudlin again.

"You're going to be much happier where you're going." That quiet, soothing voice again. "It's warmer there, too."

Fat chance. Being locked in a cage didn't

fit Catherine's definition of happy. She wrinkled her nose and cast him her iciest look.

He chuckled. "You'll thank me after you get a good meal in you." He shut the door to the car, came around to the driver's side, got in, then put the car in gear and started driving. He did a good job ignoring her plaintive wails from the seat beside him.

Nice eyes or not, she didn't want to go wherever he was taking her. She had things to do and this man, with his do-gooder, save-the-world-and-the-whales charity crusade, was getting in the way.

Catherine paced the cage, inspecting every inch. Thin metal bars, secure lock. A flat metal base, cool against her feet.

She silently cursed in English, then added a few choice words in French. The orphans had been close by, maybe five minutes from her. She'd been so focused on finding them she'd ignored the warning signals and thus, had ended up in the hands of Dr. Dolittle.

She'd rescued so many animals over the course of her lifetime — kittens, puppies, even a lost turtle once. It had become her mission, she supposed, which was ironic given that all the trouble in her life had started with saving one black cat.

Still, she wanted to find those kittens. If she could reunite them with their mother, she hoped it would give her a little more closure. Make it easier to accept the inevitable end of Catherine's life.

And then, just maybe, she'd find a taste of what she was seeking when she came to Indiana in the first place. The ordinary life. No castles. No kings. Just a house with a white picket fence and cookies in the oven.

The problem was getting away before her "rescuer" took her home and made her over into his pretty pet by stringing pink ribbons and a silver bell around her neck.

"Here we are," he said cheerily a minute later, as if he'd just pulled up outside Buckingham Palace. "Your temporary home." She hissed, but he just chuckled again. "Ah, give it a chance, little one." He came around and opened the door. He lifted out the cage, hefted it awkwardly into one arm and carried it toward the building.

Tall and well-built, he had the muscles of a man who had worked hard in his life, not one who bench-pressed his way to perfection. The scent of him — a dark, very human scent — teased at her nose. Wood shavings, pine, a bit of sweat. And warmth.

14

Like a blanket she could cuddle into.

She would *not* feel any kind of fondness for this Humanitarian Harry who'd interrupted her quest. Once he put her down, she'd find a way to escape and be on her way faster than he could say, "God Save the Queen."

He opened the door, letting it shut behind them. There was a moment of total darkness as they traveled down a hall and into another room. He flicked a switch, sending the room into light. Catherine blinked until her eyes adjusted. The man laid the cage on a metal table in the center of a small, austere, white room. She peered through the bars, then shrank back. The sheen of stainless steel glinted back at her. Instruments. Medicines. Needles.

Panicking would do nothing but put her at a disadvantage. She held herself steady, focused on escape.

"Let's get you more comfortable, shall we?" He bent and peered into her cage.

Those eyes. Brown like a river of coffee, so kind they seemed to take her into his heart and hold her there, the way she'd always hoped home would be, but never had been, even two hundred years ago.

Catherine leaned forward, nose to the metal bars.

"Ah, there you go." He reached in a finger and stroked the bridge of her nose.

She lashed out, catching him good with one nail before he yelped and pulled back. That would teach him for kidnapping her.

Do it again, Buster, and I'll show you nine more like that one.

He chuckled and wagged his injured finger at her as if she'd been an errant child. She hissed and spat and yowled her frustration, but he merely smiled.

"You're really going to make me work to get your affection, aren't you?" He reached for the latch.

Catherine stilled. Finally. A chance to escape. She lowered her body, feigning acquiescence. He unlatched the door and reached inside, two broad warm hands at once encircling her and drawing her out of the cage. His grip was firm, secure.

Inescapable.

Catherine fought against him anyway, but he cradled her close, within the soft comfort of his sweater. A well-worn wool, washed so many times it felt rather like down. He ran a hand along her head, crooning again, saying nothing at all really, but sending a sense of calm rippling through her veins.

Against every instinct she'd honed in the

last two centuries, Catherine relaxed, snuggling into that warmth, allowing herself to relax.

Such a long, lonely road I've traveled. How nice it would be to let someone else take care of me. For just one tiny, blissful minute.

And then, she'd go back to her life. To finding the kittens. To worrying about the curse, the deadline looming over her.

A low, quiet, strange rumbling started in her throat. Catherine jerked upright. The sound stopped. The man kept stroking her head and again, she relaxed. A second later, the curious sound started again, vibrating through her as gently as the wash of a tide.

Why was *that* sound coming from her throat? What did it mean? And why did it feel so good?

"There you are, little one," he whispered, touching every nerve with what seemed such intimate knowledge of the best-feeling places, "I knew I could make you purr."

She closed her eyes and forgot momentarily about escape. Absorbing simply this man, his touch, his kindness.

A few more seconds, that's all. Then she'd —

There was a squeak. Catherine opened her eyes only to see a second, bigger cage. He'd betrayed her. She shrieked but couldn't stop him from placing her inside and shutting the door.

"I'll be back, don't worry," he said. "Sleep tight."

Catherine hissed and swatted at his retreating form. A second later, the room was plunged into darkness.

She settled onto the newspaper-covered floor and let out a heavy sigh, ignoring the bowls of food and water beside her. Oh Lord, she was tired, more tired than she could remember feeling before. Maybe because the end was near. Six more days and her fate would be sealed. For better or worse, this half existence would be over.

She only had those few days to get a taste of what life might have been like — had she been able to go down a different lane. A life that could have included a husband, children. A home of her own. She'd missed out on all of that, thanks to Hezabeth's rather warped sense of revenge. If only —

Enough self-pity. Catherine got to her feet and paced the length of the metal container, clean newspaper crunching beneath her paws. She was in a bit of a sticky wicket, to say the least.

First on the agenda was escape. She'd deal with figuring out how to get back to the kittens and the alley where she'd stashed her small reserve of cash for safe-keeping later. She'd had two hundred years to ponder her fate and hadn't reached any answers yet. Better to stay busy with the things she *could* change.

There had to be a way out. Finding a twenty-five-year-old blonde busting out of the locked two-by-three cage where he'd last seen a pale orange tabby would un-doubtedly shock Humanitarian Harry into cardiac arrest. As appealing as that idea was, Catherine pushed it aside and went back to trying to figure out how she could pick a lock with four paws and a spattering of whiskers for tools.

The clock on the wall ticked along at a steady pace. Catherine had four hours to find a way out. Four hours until she changed from a cat . . . and became a woman again.

She had until sunrise to pull off a mir-acle.

Garrett couldn't sleep. Charlie, his choc-olate Labrador, snored loudly at the end of the bed. In a corner basket, Ferdinand and

Isabel, a pair of muddled-blood cats, lay stretched out and quiet. Garrett, the only human in the room, lay on the bed, eyes open, arms crossed behind his head.

He'd come back to the house he shared with his Aunt Mabel at one in the morning. As always, he'd stopped to check on his elderly aunt, turning off the blaring TV and covering her with a blanket before heading to his own room. Up until a couple weeks ago, when Aunt Mabel had come down with a bout of pneumonia and temporarily needed more care, he'd lived in a cottage that sat on the back of her land.

When her home had been part of an estate, the little house had been the gardener's home. Ten years ago, Uncle Leo had converted it into a rental property. But when Leo died, leaving a grieving and frail Mabel alone, Garrett had moved into the cottage. Just at the right time, too, given all that had gone wrong in his life then.

Garrett rolled over and punched his pillow into a new shape, but it didn't make him any sleepier. His thoughts went back to the stray he'd found that night. She was such a tiny thing, all spit and fire. Despite her temper, she was a beautiful cat — short-haired and petite, with a pale orange coat, almost blond in color. He chuckled. Whoever took her home would need a lot of patience and cat treats to win over that grumpy girl.

Exhaustion weighed on him, but not enough to grant him sleep. His mind refused to quit, to give in and stop the reminders.

Garrett hadn't slept for more than two hours at a stretch in three years. Every time he closed his eyes, the nightmares returned, tearing at him, making him relive that horrible night again and again.

To hell with it. He got to his feet. The Monday morning sun would be up in an hour or so and then sleep would be pointless. As he'd done a thousand times before, he decided to go to the office before the rest of the world woke up. There was always work.

Ever since his last assistant had quit, he'd been running himself ragged, trying to keep up with the appointments, the shelter and the day-to-day of running his practice. Dottie, his receptionist, was a big help, but what he really needed was a second pair of hands to work with the animals. Problem was, he'd been through three assistants in the past six months.

Either he couldn't hire good help or he

didn't have the personality to keep good help. He had a feeling it was the latter.

Standing around thinking about the problem wouldn't get it solved. He needed to work on plans for expanding the shelter and hopefully come up with a strategy to convince the Lawford Community Foundation to finance his dream. Their support thus far had been barely tepid, which, admittedly, was partly his fault. He wasn't exactly a great communicator. If he was going to make his dream happen, he needed a miracle before Saturday night.

Without looking in the mirror, Garrett showered, shaved and dressed. He avoided his reflection, slipping into jeans and a light blue button-down shirt, stepping into loafers and combing his hair into the same pattern as he had for almost twenty-eight years. Minutes later, he'd fed his cats and dropped them off at the cottage for the day, then set off for the office. Charlie panted in the seat beside him, eager for work.

First thing, he'd see how that cat was doing. After tangling with her last night, he'd put off an exam until today. No sense igniting her temper more than he already had. Once she was deemed healthy, he could find her a home.

He'd miss her, despite her cranky personality. He missed every animal that left his building. *You can't keep them all,* his mother always told him, *or you'll be running a zoo instead of a veterinarian's office.*

He already had three pets, more than enough for the cottage and for his aunt's home. And here, in the office, there was always a dozen or so waiting for his attention. Between the shelter and his veterinarian practice, hundreds of animals came into his care each year.

He loved them all. Well, except for Miss Tanner's giant Doberman. What he wouldn't give for a little help with Sweet Pea, whose name had nothing to do with her description or her personality. Even Dottie feared the dog, a nearly maniacal barker who ate almost everything in sight. Garrett had to admit he dreaded Miss Tanner and Sweet Pea's annual appointment. Not to mention her continual "emergency" visits with the dog.

Where her Doberman was concerned, Miss Tanner was a canine hypochondriac.

But the rest of the animals had a piece of his heart. Maybe because they never looked at him with a touch of revulsion in their eyes, never stood there with a question they dared not ask on their lips. They responded only to his touch and his voice, as if they were blind to everything else the world judged about Garrett McAllister.

He pulled up in front of the small white building decorated with a simple sign: Garrett McAllister, DVM. The sky was beginning to turn from gray to light pink as the sun edged up the horizon.

Charlie settled onto a padded dog bed by the front door. Garrett made his way through the darkened office, knowing the path without the help of a light. He'd worked here most of his life, first with Doc West, then by himself when he bought the practice from Doc three years ago. There'd been a year when he'd lived — and worked — somewhere else, but his life had always been here. These rooms were more like home than his own. More familiar, more comforting. The place where he most belonged.

He unlocked the door to the exam room. Last night, the shelter had been full, so he'd kept the tabby here. What he'd do with her once patients started coming in and out at nine, he didn't know, but he'd figure something out. A freezing rain was predicted for tonight and he had no intentions of letting the cat wander Lawford's streets.

He flicked on the light. She was sitting on her haunches, every sense on alert. As if she'd been expecting him.

"Good morning," he said. "Did you sleep?"

She glared at him in response.

He laughed. "Neither did I." Her food bowl was untouched. "Didn't like the selections on the menu? Let's try some canned food then." He pivoted, reached for a can on the shelf and opened it into a bowl. The first signs of morning orange sky peeked through the blinds. The tabby let out a howl that sounded almost panicked. "I'm coming, I'm coming," he said, turning back toward her.

She was frantic now, pawing and gnawing at the bars, shrieking in frustration.

"It's okay, little one. It's okay."

She began to toss herself against the door of the cage. Was she in pain? Sick? Garrett rushed to unlatch the lock and thrust his free hand inside to catch her.

With a howl, she leapt past him, missing his grip by millimeters, dashing across the room and out the door he'd left ajar. She was gone in the space of a heartbeat.

"You won't get far. Not unless you can open doors, too." Garrett picked up the bowl of food and left the room, following the cat's path. The office was small and most of the doors were shut. He'd find her soon enough.

One more second and it all would have been over. Her secret discovered — in one heck of a big way.

Nothing like making a grand entrance.

She darted out of the room, down the hall and through the first open door she saw. Just in time. She could feel it beginning to happen. The tingling, the stretching and expanding of her body from cat to woman.

She braced herself, hugged against the wall, knowing the pain was coming, yet jerking away in shock when it did. It was always like this when the change started. She'd never gotten used to it, even after two hundred years.

"Here kitty, kitty," came the man's voice. She heard him tap against the plastic food bowl. "Shrimp dinner. Come and get it."

By day a woman, by night a cat. The curse can only be broken if you find a man who loves you as both a woman and a cat. Every day, Hezabeth the Witch's screeching voice echoed in Catherine's mind.

Her arms and legs began to lengthen, the cat's furry hide transforming into pale skin. Catherine closed her eyes and envisioned a quiet meadow, songbirds, blooming flowers, anything but the hideous half-animal, half-human creature she was for the next few seconds.

There was another momentary protest of pain from her body and then, finally, it was over.

Before she opened her eyes, Catherine ran a hand over her face and skin. As the end of the curse drew nearer, she worried one day it would all go horribly wrong, leaving her stuck between the two worlds and looking like some fifty-cent sideshow in the carnival.

Not today, thank God. Everything felt as it should. Human. Womanly. And then, she realized —

Naked.

"Here kitty, kitty." His voice again, closer. A few feet away.

Catherine scrambled to her feet, her eyes still unseeing — the last part of her body to adjust to the switch. In a second, she'd have her vision, but right now she was essentially blind.

How could she be so unprepared? The

first time she'd transformed, she'd been caught naked in a marketplace in London during the bustle before the holidays, with vendors scrambling to set out their wares in the early morning.

When an unclothed woman had suddenly sprung up in the middle of the square, the fishmonger had dropped his mackerel, the butcher nearly chopped off his index finger, and the ladies readying the dress shop for the day had swooned, silly bats fainting as if they'd never seen a woman without clothes before.

Ever since, Catherine had made sure she was ready for the change, whether it meant stealing clothes from a washerwoman's line or diving into a charity donation bin.

But this time, she hadn't had a second to grab anything. She stood naked and cold against the wall, her vision now a blur of colors. How would she get past him? How could she explain being here at six in the morning?

Not to mention the nudity thing.

"Kitty?" The door across the hall clicked open, then shut. "Kitty?" Closer, on the other side of the pine door. *This* pine door. And then, the knob turned.

A miracle would take more time than Catherine had.

Chapter Two

Garrett flicked the switch for the overhead light in his office, bending over as he did so he wouldn't miss the cat zipping by. His gaze swept the space in front of him, to the left, then the right. Beige carpet, the leg of a cherry desk, several crumbs from yesterday's cookies baked as a thank-you by Mrs. Crane and . . . one woman's naked foot.

He stood there for a second, blinking. *One woman's naked foot.*

His gaze traveled up. A naked foot, attached to a naked leg. Garrett jerked upright and found himself looking at a twenty-ish blonde who filled out a lab coat — his lab coat — in ways that should be illegal.

His jaw dropped open. Not a word came out.

She, however, didn't seem so surprised to see him. She smiled, a soft look that took over her face and reached into her gray-green eyes. A strange feeling of connection zipped through Garrett, which was odd, because he knew he'd never met her before. And yet, he felt as if he *should* know her.

"I'm so pleased to meet you, Dr. —" her gaze flicked to his desk, then back. She sounded slightly out of breath, which caused a weird hitch in Garrett's own breathing. "Dr. McAllister. I've been anxious to talk to you."

"What are you doing in my office? Wearing *my* lab coat?"

"I told you. I wanted to talk to you."

He could barely get his mind around any of this. "What? Why?"

If she had on any clothes at all, they were very short and hidden by the knee-length white jacket. Either way, he couldn't focus on anything but the creamy length of her legs and the way the oversized jacket dipped in front, giving him a too-brief peek at the rounded pale curves of her breasts.

"I, umm . . . I wanted to talk to you about ah . . . a . . . job." She gave a quick, firm nod.

He quirked an eyebrow. "A job?"

"As your . . . assistant. You know, helping with the animals." The smile again, secure, confident.

Had he been in some kind of fugue state yesterday and forgotten he'd hired her?

No, impossible. He'd never forget hiring a woman like her. Besides, people didn't exactly clamor to work for him. His last two assistants had said he lacked any kind of people skills before they'd slammed the door and left for good. Not to mention that most of his annual budget was poured into keeping the shelter up and running.

Although he needed the help, he preferred to work alone. Dealing with people was a hell of a lot harder than dealing with animals. People asked questions. People stared. People, he'd found, could disappoint you and let you down when you needed them most.

He'd already been down that road one painful time too many.

"I don't have an opening for an assistant right now." Another glimpse of her legs, then his gaze traveled up to her lean, heart-shaped face and deep gray-green eyes. "At least, I don't think I do."

A slow smile spread across her face like peanut butter on toast. Her gaze locked on his, and she took a step forward. "A busy vet can always use more help, I'm sure."

He gestured at her, a hundred questions

in the movement of his hands. "How did you get in here?"

"That's rather a long story," she said.

He crossed his arms over his chest and leaned against the doorjamb. "I have time."

"Well . . ." Her voice trailed off. She bit her lip and took a step back, settling on the corner of his desk. When she sat, the lab coat rode up, exposing more of her thighs.

His heart rate leapt to five times the normal rate. Garrett swallowed and forced his jaw to stay in place this time. Maybe this was one of those reality show pranks where someone had set him up with a gorgeous woman pretending she wanted a job.

"I . . ." she glanced around the room again, then back at him. "I was here late yesterday to talk to you about a job, but you'd already left. Your receptionist said I could find you here early in the morning. I got ah, turned around when I went to leave and accidentally got locked in."

"It's a small building. Not exactly full of halls and wrong turns."

"I was nervous."

She looked like the kind of woman who never got flustered. Her story had more holes than a cheap pair of socks. And yet, he sensed a vulnerability about her, as if

she wasn't used to asking for help or re-
lying on others. Much like himself, he realized. And for some odd reason, that made
him want to help her.

He needed more sleep. Clearly, he
wasn't thinking straight.

"I didn't see you when I came back late
last night," he said.

"I fell asleep in your chair. When I'm
asleep, the Macy's Thanksgiving Day Pa-
rade could come by and I'd never hear a
thing."

"Must be nice to sleep that deeply," he
said quietly, then drew himself up. He
wasn't here to confess his insomnia problems to a stranger, especially one without
any clothes on.

The way the coat drifted over her and
peaked above her breasts, he suspected she
was nude. Completely nude.

Oh boy, was he going to have a lot of
fantasies running through his head over
this one. He'd never look at that coat the
same way again. "Do you, ah, always dress
like this for a job interview?"

"I . . . I spilled some coffee on my
clothes last night and washed them out in
the sink. I slipped on this to wear until
they dried. I didn't expect you to be here
so early. I hope you don't mind." She

crossed one leg over the other, which only served to hitch the coat up farther.

He gulped. "Uh . . . no."

She smiled again. "Good."

"Did it hit your shoes, too?"

"Shoes?"

He looked pointedly at her bare feet.

"Oh, ah, yeah. Coffee all over them."

"Must have been a hell of a big mug."

She nodded quickly. Too quickly. "Huge."

He should send her packing. Mentally, Garrett started ticking through the inconsistencies in her tale. "Why —"

"Well, let's get to work," she said, interrupting him with an enthusiastic clap. "I bet the animals are starving."

"I don't need an assistant."

"I find that hard to believe. There are lots of animals here. You definitely need help."

"I can't afford an assistant. I can barely afford me."

"I'll work for peanuts."

She had an argument for his every reason not to hire her. "But —" he tried one last time, sputtering like an engine that couldn't quite quit.

"Give me a trial run this morning and if I don't work out, I'll take off your lab coat and leave you alone. Sound fair?"

A mental image of her stripping off his jacket popped unbidden into Garrett's mind. For a second, he considered firing her just to see her remove it and walk out the door.

She would never do. For one, she was too distracting. For another, she was much too pleasant to be working with him. He'd have to be nice, and that was something Garrett rarely succeeded at.

"I don't work well with other people hovering around me," he said.

"You won't even know I'm here. I'll be quiet as a cat." She winked.

He thought of the dozens of patients that would be in and out today. The paperwork still sitting on his desk that he hadn't gotten to in weeks. The stack of unreturned phone messages. The supplies list he needed to go over. The records he needed to finish updating. Not to mention the three dozen animals currently residing in the shelter.

And today was Miss Tanner's annual visit with Sweet Pea. That alone was enough reason to bring in reinforcements.

He wasn't about to admit it, but the stranger in his office had impeccable timing.

"Okay, I'll try you out today. But," he

held up a finger before she could say anything, "just today."

She beamed. "Great! I love working with animals."

"You might want to —" he gestured at her, not knowing what words to use.

"Want to what?"

"Ah, put something on beneath the coat."

"Oh." She blushed, and the red extended down her chest, flushing bright against the white fabric. "My clothes probably won't be dry for hours. Any chance you have something in a size eight here?"

He thought of telling her to just go buy something, but the thought of her parading down the street in nothing more than his lab coat stopped him. "Try the storage room. Tiffany probably left a few things there."

"Tiffany?"

"Assistant number three. She had a backup closet of clothes here in case she wanted to change." Garrett scowled. "When she quit, she left pretty fast. And left behind part of her wardrobe."

"Why'd she quit?"

"We had a disagreement over which kind of mammals Tiffany should be tending to."

The woman raised her eyes.

"Tiffany had more interest in creatures with two legs than the ones with four."

"Oh." She paused, then her mouth opened. *"Oh."*

Garrett shifted on his feet. The room seemed awfully warm. Furnace must be on the blink again.

Yeah, that was it.

"I have to get to work," he said. He went to reach for the hook that normally held his lab coat, realized where it was, and jerked his hand back. Without a second glance at the woman or his jacket, Garrett turned on his heel and left the room.

He headed down the hall, looking for the cat that had escaped his grasp that morning but he didn't see her anywhere. Odd how she had disappeared like that. Usually, Charlie would have tracked down any strays running around the office, but there was no sign of the sassy feline from last night.

Garrett entered the shelter and went first to the animals that needed him most. They were the abandoned and unwanted pets society forgot. Garrett found most people never gave a second thought to strays — unless they were messing up the front lawn.

That attitude was what he was fighting

against in his quest to get funding for a bigger shelter. So far, he'd had no success. If things didn't work out on Saturday, he wasn't sure what he was going to do. His building was too small to house more than a few dogs and cats. And there were so many, more than one office could hold.

With more money, he could hire help, expand the space, make a difference. And maybe, just maybe, find a little peace. He'd spent the last three years working himself to death and that hadn't brought him one inch of serenity. Maybe if the shelter were a success and he could save just a few more animals, Garrett could regain a little of what he'd lost in that fire.

He turned on the light, dimmed the switch to gently light the room. "Hey, Rags," he crooned to a motley-colored dog in the first kennel. The mutt leapt to his feet, tail wagging furiously. He let out a few yips and pressed his nose to the kennel's bars. Garrett chuckled and rubbed Rags's nose with two fingers. "I'll feed you in a second. Let me check on the others."

He moved down the line, greeting each animal in turn. He'd given them all names, humanizing each a little bit. Most were as excited to see him as children at Christmas.

Except one. In the last cage, a thin white cat sat on her haunches, nose in the air, seeming to ignore him even though she was looking straight ahead. "Hi, Queenie," he said. "You gonna look at me today?"

She raised her nose more, stood, turned three quarters of the way around, and gave him her back.

"You're one tough cookie." He reached forward, testing the waters. He'd never gotten very far with Queenie, a stray he'd found a week ago. She had the personality of a wolverine and clearly didn't appreciate his gestures of kindness or his presence.

Someone must have been very cruel to her at one time. It would probably be a while before she stopped hating everything human.

When his hand was three inches from the cage, Queenie whirled around, hissing and batting at the bars.

A long while, he amended.

"Okay, we'll try again later." Garrett frowned. Her food bowl was still untouched. "That's three days, Missy. You can't go on a hunger strike." She hissed some more. He shook his head. He couldn't save them all.

But, Lord, how he wanted to.

He walked back to the dog kennels and

started collecting food bowls, avoiding more than one eager puppy tackle as he made his way in and out of the cages.

He knew she was there without even turning around. He sensed her standing behind him, silent and watching. He stumbled with one of the bowls, spilling kibble on the floor outside a spaniel's kennel.

She was beside him in an instant, dustpan in hand. Still wearing just the damned lab coat, too. "Let me get that for you."

"I can do it," he grumbled. He yanked the dustpan out of her grip and scooped up the dry dog food, dumping it into a bin.

"I'm supposed to be your assistant. Let me assist."

He busied himself with measuring food into the other bowls, avoiding her gaze. "You could have at least gotten dressed, for God's sake."

"I am dressed. Besides, you didn't tell me where the storage room was. I didn't think you'd want me wandering around your building, poking in all the rooms." She took the dustpan and hung it back on its hook. "The animals are probably starving. I'll change after we feed them."

He whirled around, careful to keep his face out of the direct light. "Why do you keep insisting on taking this job?"

"I like peanuts." She smiled. When she spoke again, her voice was softer. "Mostly, because I love animals. I like working with them. I've always wanted to work in a vet's office, but —" She shrugged, as if the ending of the sentence wasn't important, but he got the feeling that it was quite the opposite.

Over the years, Garrett had gotten very good at telling which camp most people were in: animal lover, hater or indifferent. She was clearly in the first group. He respected that, very much. Even so, he wasn't sure he could afford to hire her, nor did he really want someone underfoot all day.

"Face it. I'm a perfect fit for you," she said.

"There are thousands of other veterinarians. Why do you keep bothering me?"

"Because I'm already here. And because you need an assistant more than anyone else I know." She put her hands on her hips and the jacket rose, exposing more of her thighs.

Garrett held tight to the bowl before he scattered kibble at her feet like some pathetic gift to the goddess.

"Listen," she began. "I'll work for free today. Then you don't lose anything. If it

41

works out, great. Keep me here. If it doesn't, I'll be on my way. No loss, no hard feelings."

A twinge of disappointment ran through him at the thought of her walking out the door. That was crazy. He barely knew the woman. And besides, she annoyed the heck out of him. She'd shown up at the worst possible time, disrupting his day, his schedule and making him act like a clumsy five-year-old.

He had a hundred reasons why it wouldn't work out. Another dozen why her leaving would be best. For both of them.

But all his excuses seemed to get stuck in the back of his brain. "I don't even know your name."

"Catherine Wyndham." She thrust out a hand.

He took her hand. Long fingers, skin as soft as satin, a touch as delicate as cashmere.

She hadn't flinched when her palm met his scarred one. He'd never met anyone who could touch him without even a flicker of attention toward the marks on his skin. It was as if he were himself again, before —

He quickly let go. "Garrett McAllister."

"Pleased to meet you, Doctor Mc—"

"If you insist on staying here, make yourself useful." He waved at the white cat's cage. Start the woman off with a tough assignment first and maybe she'd give up. "Try to get Queenie to eat something." Garrett grabbed a bag of moist cat food off the shelf. "This one has extra vitamins. She's a little thin." He thrust the bag at her, but she was already gone, her hands inside Queenie's cage.

"I wouldn't do that if I were you. She's . . . testy."

"This cat?" Catherine smiled. "She's sweet." She cradled Queenie close to her chest and whispered something into the cat's ear. Queenie shot Garrett a look of disdain, then settled into Catherine's arms.

And started to purr.

"How the hell did you do that?"

"Do what?"

"Get her to play nice."

Catherine shrugged. "I have a way with cats."

"A touch of magic is more like it," he muttered. "That cat hates me."

"You just have to know how to talk to her." Catherine scratched behind Queenie's ear. The cat practically moaned.

"I know how to treat animals. I'm a vet, remember?"

"You're also a human. That puts you in a different category from her right from the start."

He raised an eyebrow. "Are you saying you're not human?"

She looked away. "Can you, ah, pour the cat food for me?" Catherine hoisted the cat in her arms. "It's a little hard to juggle both."

"Oh yeah. Sure." Only one of his brain cells seemed to be firing. He'd already forgotten the cat in her arms. All he'd seen for the past couple minutes were Catherine's gray-green eyes, so wide, so observant. He'd seen eyes that color once before, but for the life of him, he couldn't remember where.

Garrett turned back to the counter and filled a bowl with the moist food. He flaked the meaty nuggets with a fork, then pivoted to give the bowl to Catherine.

She took a step forward and reached for the dish. When she did, her hand brushed his. His remaining brain cell sputtered to a stop.

"Thanks." Her lips curved in another smile. He couldn't remember the last time a woman had smiled at him like *that*.

Garrett's heart gave a jerky lurch.

The only response he could muster up

came out more like half a grunt than a word. He whirled back to the counter, measuring medicines into cups and syringes.

Concentrate on work, not on the woman standing five feet behind him and wearing his lab coat in ways that a lab coat should never be worn.

"Doctor McAllister —"

"I have to check on the other animals." He left the room before he lost the capacity to breathe.

The woman was trouble, without a doubt. The sooner she was gone, the better.

Catherine watched the hurried, retreating figure of Garrett McAllister. So like a human. Heck, so like a male.

"Us girls should stick together, huh?" she said to the cat, placing Queenie and her food back into the cage. A final pat, then she left the feline to her meal. Something was bothering Queenie, but when Catherine had tried to read her, the cat had shut down and blocked out any attempt to communicate. Ever since the curse, she'd been able to "talk" to other animals in a silent manner. Sort of a mental telepathy that had helped her find a good place to sleep, a meal when she needed one and her way to a new temporary home. But now, as the end of the curse approached, those powers were weaker. Catherine decided to try again later. "I'll be back in a little bit."

Catherine stood in the center of the room. Should she follow him? She was, after all, supposed to be proving herself as his assistant, which meant actually assisting. He hadn't given her anything to do, but then again, he didn't seem the type to ask for help.

She wrinkled up her nose, ran through twenty reasons why she should not chase after a cranky veterinarian who wanted nothing to do with her, then headed out the door and down the hall to the second set of kennels.

As she walked, she realized Garrett could be useful.

Her tracking skills had grown weaker as the years passed, her instincts less sharp, as if her feline abilities weakened as the curse's end neared. She'd seen it when she'd tried to connect with Queenie and been blocked.

As a human, she had little. No money, no clothes, no transportation. As a cat, even less.

Finding the kittens was going to be difficult. She wanted to find them, one last rescue before she couldn't rescue anyone anymore. She wasn't sure what would happen when the curse ended, but she was sure many of her telepathic gifts would disappear. She had to help those orphans at least. Because if there was anything Catherine understood, it was being without a family. The trio could be anywhere by now, though chances were good they'd stick close to where she'd last seen them. Wherever that might be. She'd lost all sense of direction during the midnight car ride. They could be thirty blocks or thirty miles away.

Finding her way to the white-picket-fence life for the last few days of her human existence would be even more impossible. She'd lived in castles, in spacious mansions with rich people who never noticed her, thinking *that* was the life. But it wasn't. As she got older, Catherine realized the one thing she craved was the one thing she'd never had — simplicity. What had she been thinking when she'd come up with that crazy idea? She hadn't been thinking. She'd simply hopped a bus and headed for the Midwest, getting off just before sunset yesterday.

No plan, no idea how she was going to accomplish this. Just an overwhelming urge to taste that one bit of life left unsavored.

She hated to admit it, but she could use a helping hand. Someone who knew animals, knew the city and could help her find what she needed before the sun set on Saturday.

That someone could very well be Garrett McAllister, whether he liked it or not.

She heard his voice before she reached the room. The same soft reassuring tones he'd used on her last night. With animals, he was clearly at ease. With people —

Well, he had the personality of a grumpy grizzly.

Catherine could understand. She'd never been much of a people person herself, even less so in the two hundred years since she'd been cursed to spend her days as a drifter and her nights as a cat.

That kind of life gave a woman a whole new appreciation for other species, particularly the kind with fur. And a new vision of the humans who too often saw animals as disposable. Catherine had long ago realized the way a man treated his pets was often a good indication of how he'd treat other people.

Garrett, however, didn't fit that theory. He was caring and tender with animals; prickly and annoyed with people. Last night, though, he'd been kind and gentle. He'd treated her well, as if he cared about what happened to her. No one had acted like that with her before, especially not when she'd been in feline form.

Perhaps he understood what it was like to be a stray, on the fringes of the ordinary, pretty, "groomed" world. He always kept his face turned slightly away from her whenever they talked, as if he didn't want her to look at him.

In his office, he'd stayed in the shadows of the hall, and then here, in the shelter, the lights had been dimmed and Garrett had kept his back to her most of the time.

Keeping the scars from view, she suspected. He was an outsider, just like she was. Maybe . . .

No, that was a crazy thought.

On Saturday, none of this would matter anymore either way. The curse would end and she'd be left forever as a cat. She had five more sunsets, six more sunrises and then . . . it would be over.

Before that happened, she had one last hurrah to live. She'd already traveled the world. Seen the sights, met the kings. All she wanted now was a taste of the ordinary. Of waking up in one place day after day. Feeding the birds in the morning and watching the sun set on a back porch. Such simple things, but for a woman who had spent her life going from place to place, century to century, it was the only thing she craved.

And she had to find those kittens. To give one more happy ending to a set of young strays.

Catherine sighed. She had a lot to accomplish by Saturday. Changing Garrett McAllister's life was *not* on that list.

Then why did she suddenly find herself at the door to the kennels? It wasn't just because she wanted to work as a vet's assistant. There was more.

She'd known since the first moment he'd caught her and held her close with kindness and trust. There'd been something in his eyes, something indefinable.

A connection.

Try as she might, she couldn't ignore that invisible tether.

She found him working with an older golden retriever. He had already folded up the sleeves of his pale blue shirt and flipped his navy and red striped tie over his shoulder to keep it out of the way. He looked so at ease, so comfortable, with his dark wavy hair slightly messy and his hands capably handling the dog. This was clearly where Garrett was most at home.

"There's a pile of bandages over there if you want to help," he said without turning around.

She grabbed the bandages and crossed to him. White cotton strips ran across the opposite flank of the dog. The dog's fur had faded and paled in some spots and she limped a little as she sidled up to Garrett. "Is she hurt?"

"Nah, just thinks she's still a puppy." He gave the dog a tender caress. She nuzzled him back. "She raced a squirrel and lost. Hit a tree with her hip and scraped it up pretty bad."

When he reached to take the bandages, his hand brushed hers. A jolt rushed through her and Catherine drew back. Garrett turned away, busied with applying the new bandage.

Had he been as affected as she? Had he felt that . . . that electrical shock?

It was her feet against the carpet. Static electricity. Yeah, except her feet were bare and they were standing on vinyl flooring.

The light was streaming through the windows now, exposing his face clearly.

She saw the jagged lines that ran down his face, disappearing under his neckline, almost like pale pink zippers running along his cheeks and neck. The backs of his hands were scarred as well, dark red in some places, soft cherry in others.

Something terrible had happened to Garrett McAllister. Something he seemed to want to hide, judging by the way he kept his face averted and avoided looking directly at her.

Garrett led the retriever back to her kennel, giving her another gentle pat and a few kind words before closing the door and moving on to a small multicolored Pekingese. His hand hovered over the latch, his back to her. "This isn't going to work, Miss Wyndham. Maybe you should find other employment."

She crossed the room in three strides, coming to a stop beside him. "What do you mean?"

"I don't work well with others."

She softened her tone. "Because of your scars?"

He wheeled around, a volcano erupting in his eyes. "Who do you think you are? How dare you come in here and start intruding on my life?"

She took a step back, speechless.

"I didn't ask you for a commentary on my appearance. I asked you to *leave*."

"Leave?"

"Yeah, and the sooner the better." He turned back to the kennel, but didn't unlatch the door. The Pekingese yipped impatiently.

Bloody hell. Catherine stood there, facing his back for several seconds, chewing on her lip. She needed his help, but there was no way she was asking for it now. She'd never before needed a man to help her do anything.

She wasn't about to start now.

"Your wish is my command." She stripped off the lab coat, then reached over his head and dangled it in front of his face. The muscles in his neck flexed and tensed when he swallowed. Twice. He stared at the coat as if he'd never seen it before. She dropped it on the top of the kennel. The Pekingese barked at the pile of fabric. "I'm gone."

Then she turned on her naked heel and left the room, certain Garrett would be spending the next few minutes picking his jaw up off the floor.

Chapter Three

Garrett remained rooted to the spot until he heard the soft whoosh of the door. Then, when he could function enough to move, he took a seat on the rolling stool in the corner. He left the lab coat on the kennel, an empty reminder of the woman who'd just been wearing it.

His mind conjured up several pictures of the retreating and naked Catherine but he dismissed them all, trying his damnedest not to think about what she looked like without his jacket.

It worked, for about one second, and then the pictures came anyway. Luscious, creamy skin. Firm thighs and breasts. And above it all, those steady gray-green eyes, watching him.

Garrett closed his eyes, leaned against the wall. He'd done the right thing by getting rid of Catherine Wyndham.

Then he thought of Queenie, and how

she'd responded to the woman's touch. How the dogs seemed to calm when she walked by. How every animal in the place appeared to watch her, as if they knew her somehow.

He'd never met anyone who had such a connection with animals. She would have made the perfect assistant. An even better vet.

For someone else, he amended. Not for him.

And yet, he couldn't rejoice at driving her away, as he had all the other times he'd made someone leave him alone. By asking about his scars, she'd opened the door most polite people left shut. Everyone else was smart enough to leave it at staring and whispering about him behind his back, wondering what tragedy had left him with that tortured appearance.

There were rumors, Garrett knew. A vengeful woman who'd set his house on fire. A drunken night of partying ending in a fiery car wreck. A fight with another man over a girlfriend. The whispers were constant. Garrett didn't bother to correct anyone. His scars were his own mark of stupidity and he saw no reason to tell anyone about how he'd earned them.

Still, he'd been mean to her — too mean.

He'd lashed out like a dog that had been beaten and didn't know a gentle hand from a cruel one. Somewhere in the last three years, he'd lost the bridge to people and replaced it with one to animals. Clearly, he'd gotten to the point where he couldn't even behave like a civilized person anymore.

At the very least, he owed Catherine Wyndham an apology.

He heard another door open and close, somewhere in the back. She must have gone in search of Tiffany's clothes. Despite his best intentions, he pictured her slipping into a dress, the silky fabric gliding over her breasts, sliding past her waist, snuggling along her hips. Touching where his hands dared not go.

He'd been alone for so long. Three long years spent in an empty, cold bed. Three long years without the voice of another. With only his own company, which admittedly, wasn't all that pleasant.

Garrett stood and went down the hall, toward the storeroom. He raised his hand to knock on the door, but she opened it before his knuckles met the wood. "I'm leaving now. You don't have to escort me out the door."

Tiffany apparently hadn't left many clothing choices behind. Nor had she been as tall as Catherine. The skirt Catherine wore only reached her mid-thigh, the black suede against the pale expanse of her skin. She wore a fuzzy pink sweater that rode up a little on her stomach, exposing a flat, pretty abdomen. And on her feet, red high heels that did nothing to calm the fantasies rolling through his mind.

"I'm not here to throw you out. I just came to —" His words drained away when she shifted and the sweater strained against her rib cage.

Tiffany had definitely been smaller than Catherine. In every way.

The slide show of her in the nude and in his bed played again in his mind, a lusty tape stuck on repeat. If he'd had a mental Pause button, he wasn't so sure he'd have the strength to punch it.

Silence ticked between them. "Came to . . . what?"

He cleared his throat, reminded himself of his real reason for coming down this hall. "Apologize," he muttered.

"Did I hear you say *apologize* or *antagonize?*"

"Hey, I came to say I was sorry, not start a fight."

She put her hands on her hips and the sweater jumped up another inch. Oh Lord, she had an innie. A petite, perfect belly button.

He needed a drink.

"Then say it," she said.

He let out a gust that mixed a hundred different types of frustration into one. "I'm sorry."

"Thank you." She gave him a curt nod. "Have a nice life."

Catherine brushed past him to leave and he caught her arm. The move sent her off-kilter and she stumbled back, against his chest. The link he'd felt earlier with her multiplied tenfold, launching within him like a burst of color in a black and white world.

So many years. So lonely.

Before he could think about what he was doing, he leaned forward and kissed her.

So many years. So lonely.

The words echoed in Catherine's head. Had she thought them? Or had he?

When Garrett touched her, a searing heat exploded within her veins. Instead of pulling away, Catherine drew closer, seeking, needing . . .

What, she didn't know.

And then . . . and then, his lips met hers and she knew what she needed. This —

this touch, this tender, reverent touch, drifting over her mouth with the care of a jeweler handling a rare diamond.

She opened her mouth to his, ignoring the warning bells going off in her head, heeding only the strange desire for more of whatever was between them. She twisted against him, pressing herself to his torso, her hands reaching for his back. He cupped her face, rough skin against smooth, so full of sensation it seemed like a thousand nerve endings were awakening for the first time.

So many years, with no physical contact from others. She'd done her best to stay distant, to keep her heart intact, knowing she'd just be moving on again. But here, with Garrett's mouth on hers, his hand against her cheeks, her chest pressed to his, she felt . . .

She felt as if she'd come home.

From the other room, a cat let out a meow. The sound jerked Catherine back to reality. To her damned half existence.

The curse can only be broken if you can find a man who can love you both as a woman and as a cat, the witch had said. That evil twist on the fairy tale — the witch knew what she'd been doing. No one could love her knowing she was half human and half house pet.

Even this man, with his clear love for animals, would recoil if he knew what she really was. What she became when the sun went down.

She stumbled back, breaking the connection. Her breath hitched in her throat. She pressed a hand to her heart, willing it to slow. "That shouldn't have happened. I'm sorry."

"Don't apologize. I was completely at fault. I —" He swallowed hard and took two steps back, once again hiding his face from her in the shadow of the corner, as if the intimacy of their kiss had opened another wound. "It's best if you leave."

"Yes . . . yes it is." Yet for a second, she remained where she stood. Despite her vow to stay away from relationships, she craved more of what they'd just shared.

Garrett's eyes met hers for one brief second, then he turned away and disappeared through the double lobby doors and back into the office without a word.

Catherine watched him go, disappointment churning in her stomach like curdled cream. Before she could do something really stupid — like go after him and pick up where they'd left off — she turned on her heel and headed for the door.

When she reached the bright, harsh morning light and the busy street, she remembered her predicament. She was stuck in a strange city with no money, no transportation and no idea of where she needed to go. She'd just ditched the sole immediate job prospect she had, then gone and kissed the only man in town who'd offered her one, muddying the waters with all the finesse of a water buffalo.

And all before lunch.

Not to mention she was wearing these horrendous three-inch heels, a skirt that covered little more than her behind, and a sweater that seemed ready to unravel at the least gust of wind. In her haste, she'd forgotten to grab a coat and the November air took full advantage, seeping through her meager clothes and gnawing at her skin.

Why hadn't she picked Florida? Or California? Or maybe even Bali? Surely they had homes with white picket fences there, too. Anywhere but Indiana, the middle of nowhere, in the latter part of fall.

Catherine stood on the sidewalk outside Garrett's office, unsure of which direction to go. Her stomach let out a rumbling reminder that she hadn't eaten since dinner the day before. The money she'd earned at her last job — waitressing in a diner in

Amarillo — had been enough to pay for her trip here and a week's worth of meals. She'd stashed the money behind a loose brick in the alley yesterday, but now it seemed a million miles away.

That was how she'd lived her life for nearly two centuries. A different town, a different job, enough to eat and live a bit, then she'd be back on the move again, seeking something — anything — that would fill this endless hunger in her belly.

Making money had been easy. There was always an employer willing to save a few tax dollars by paying her under the table. But after a while, her lack of an identity created more than a few problems.

Like a driver's license. The DMV, Catherine suspected, would have a few questions if she told them she'd been born June fourth . . . in 1779. They'd probably lock her up in Bellevue and throw away the key.

Not that she had ever learned to drive — the advent of cars had been one of the big surprises to her in the last two centuries — but if she could, someday, she dreamed of sitting behind one of those machines and traveling the miles faster than she could blink.

"Here. I thought you might need this."

Catherine wheeled around. Garrett stood behind her, holding a fuchsia faux fur coat. She almost laughed at the incongruous sight of the shirt-and-tie vet clutching a hot pink coat worthy of a brothel. "Another Tiffany donation?"

"She had strange tastes." He draped the coat over her shoulders. Then he came around to face her, his eyes appraising. "I didn't see your clothes anywhere inside."

Catherine fumbled for a reasonable lie. "I — I —" she came up empty.

His gaze narrowed. "Where are you from anyway?"

She looked away. "Everywhere."

"What are you, an escaped convict? Serial murderer on the lam?"

"If I told you, you'd never believe me." She fastened the two buttons on the front of the coat and then thrust out her hand. "Thank you for the coat and the clothes, Dr. McAllister. I'll be sure to return it tomorrow. I'm sorry for bothering you today."

Garrett ignored her hand. "You're lying to me."

"Lying? I'm not lying. I really am quite sorry."

"No, about this whole thing. How you ended up here. Naked. In my office. With no car, no purse, no shoes. And no money, I presume?" When she didn't answer the question, he crossed his arms and leaned against the building. "I should call the police and let them deal with you."

"Don't." She reached again for him, but the sour expression on his face made her draw back. *"Please."*

He cocked his head, studying her. "I shouldn't help you."

She threw up her hands. "Then don't. I'm leaving anyway. I won't bother you again." She turned on her heel, took several teetering steps forward. The vise-grip shoes pinched at her toes.

"I said I *shouldn't* help you. I didn't say I wouldn't." She paused. The words sank in and she pivoted. He waved her toward the door. "Get back inside. It's too cold to debate this on the sidewalk."

The temperature was hovering in the forties and the miniskirt and waist-length jacket combo did little to keep the fall air out. Her feet had started to cramp and she felt a little faint from lack of food.

Plus, she had no idea where she was going. Delaying her departure for a few seconds of warmth seemed a rather smart idea. He opened the door and she stepped inside.

The door creaked shut behind them and the building's heat wrapped around her. The man didn't skimp on utilities.

Garrett looked at the tiled floor, as if he were considering something, then back up again at her. Their eyes met and held. Catherine could almost hear him working through what he was going to do with her.

She had no doubt he was capable of calling the police. If he did, she'd end up spending at least some of her remaining days in jail. No ID, no home, no one to vouch for her. There'd be the inevitable questions, fingerprints and background checks. Catherine knew the routine. She'd been through it a half a dozen times.

But the man she'd met last night, the one who'd cradled her close and given her a warm bed and a bowl of food, was a very different man. The kind who rescued strays and found them homes instead of leaving them to fend for themselves. The kind of man who had a soft spot for a lonely, cold animal with nowhere to go.

She could only hope she was dealing with the latter.

"Listen," he began, his gaze never leaving hers, as if he were still making up his mind as he talked, "Miss Tanner's going to be here soon. She's always on time and she's always the first appointment. Help me with Sweet Pea and I'll pay you for your time. Then you can leave, if you want."

"Are you asking me for help?"

He scowled. "I'm giving you a job. Isn't that what you wanted in the first place?"

"Well, yes."

"Good." He cleared his throat, then his voice dropped a pitch or two. "You know, you're better than Tiffany ever was."

A compliment. He must really be desperate for help.

"Better with the four-legged mammals?" She smiled at him. "Or the two-legged ones?"

He ran a hand through his hair and let out a gust. "Are you taking the job or not?"

Oh, to be around animals all day, helping the new ones come into the world, tending to the sick, comforting the dying. It was the exact type of job she'd always wanted — and never had.

Surely, a few hours here wouldn't hurt anything and maybe, she could turn her helping him into an advantage. "If I do, I need a favor in return," she said.

"You're asking me for a favor? Aren't

you the one with no clothes, no shoes, no car and no home?"

"You're the one with a Sweet Pea and no assistant." She pivoted and reached for the door handle.

"All right. What's the favor?" The words came out almost like a growl.

"There are some kittens I need to find. They've become separated from their mother and they're too young to be out on their own. I had almost caught them myself when you —"

"When I what?"

"When you-you-Ulysses got in my way." A lame save, but it was all she could come up with.

"Ulysses?" He quirked a brow at her. "You know someone named Ulysses?"

The door swung open and a small, spry elderly lady dressed in a hunter-green jumper hustled in, toting a plastic container. "Hi, Doc!" She turned and swung her wool coat off her shoulders and onto the hall tree. "Do you remember what today is? I brought some biscuits to tame the wild beast —" She stopped when she noticed Catherine five feet away. "Why, hello. Who are you?"

Catherine smiled. The woman was already easy to like. "Catherine Wyndham,

Dr. McAllister's new assistant."

"New assistant? Great!" The other woman smiled. "I'm Dottie Wilbur. Receptionist for the doc here. I only work Monday through Thursday from eight to four, so if he needs something on Friday . . ."

"I call her anyway," Garrett deadpanned.

"He does indeed." Dottie leaned forward and cupped a hand around her mouth, whispering loudly to Catherine. "He tells me it's because he can never remember what day it is, but I think he gets lonely for my conversation."

"I do *not* get lonely."

Dottie raised her brows at him. "Yeah, you can really have a great one-on-one with a Labrador, can't you?"

"Dottie . . ."

She toodled a wave and headed for the front desk. "His bark is worse than his bite," she said to Catherine as she passed. "He's actually a pretty nice guy."

"Don't go spreading rumors," Garrett said.

"I figure if I say it often enough, you'll actually become one." She winked at him, then settled herself behind the desk, tapping papers into neat, precise piles.

Garrett realized there hadn't been a single spark of recognition between Dottie and Catherine. "I thought you said you talked to my receptionist yesterday," he said, taking a stance against the wall again and crossing his arms on his chest. "She didn't seem to remember you."

"Well . . . I sort of didn't talk to her."

"Sort of?" He cocked his head. "What does that mean?"

She put her hands on her hips. Geez, didn't the woman know what happened with her shirt and jacket when she did that? A thin sliver of pale, smooth skin peeked out from beneath the too-short clothes, a perfect crescent moon.

There went his blood pressure again. Five more minutes with her and he'd need an oxygen tank.

"What did that kiss mean earlier?" she said.

He dragged his gaze back up to her face. He didn't know what that kiss had meant, beyond a moment of insanity. A *very* nice moment. One that reminded him of what life had been like before he'd become a scarred, bitter shell of a man. If he could have, he would have bottled that moment to keep on his nightstand for those endless nights when sleep hovered just outside his grasp. "You can't answer a question with a question."

"Says who?"

"Me."

"And who do you think you are?"

"Your boss, remember?"

"Oh, so now you're employing me? I thought this was a temporary, one-patient gig." She still had her hands on her hips and it was taking a considerable amount of effort for Garrett to focus on anything else.

"I'll keep you on as long as I can stand you," he said.

"That goes both ways, you know."

"It does." His arms relaxed and his gaze roved over her, despite his best intentions. Lord help him, but all he wanted to do was kiss her. Again. And again, until he forgot this world and saw only hers. He wanted to recapture that fleeting moment. Like a flutter of hope tingling between them.

"It certainly does," he said softly, not even sure what he meant.

She opened her mouth to answer him, then shut it without saying a word. Her gray-green eyes zeroed in on his. The connection tethered between them again, stronger. He felt as if there were some cosmic message he was supposed to be getting, but he had no idea what it might be.

He'd forgotten to eat breakfast. That's all. Euphoria brought on by near starvation.

"I think we have a problem," Catherine said.

Garrett nodded. "Yeah, I agree. A big one."

"A big brown one," she said. "And it's coming this way."

It took Garrett a second, then he connected the words with her gestures at the door and the enormous barking beast coming up the walkway. "That? That's not a problem. That's Sweet Pea. Meet your first patient, Miss Wyndham."

Chapter Four

The dog barged through the double lobby doors. Catherine shrank back against the wall, sure the monstrous beast intended to devour her. She'd never been more grateful to be in human form. As a cat, the Doberman would have seen her as a midnight snack.

"Sweet Pea," Garrett said in Catherine's ear, his breath warm against her neck, almost a tickle of a touch, "is neither sweet nor pea-sized, but don't let Miss Tanner know you think that."

At the end of the taut leash came a woman, probably in her early seventies. She was dressed in jeans and a sweatshirt and wore tan hiking boots, undoubtedly for traction.

Her hair was a short shock of gray and stuck out in haphazard strands around her head. It wasn't hard to tell who was in charge — the boisterous dog or the woman he carried at the end of his leash.

"Hello, Miss Tanner," Garrett said, stepping forward. He took the leash from her and with a quick jerk, brought Sweet Pea back to her haunches. The dog let out several booming barks in protest. "Here for your appointment? Already?"

"Of course."

"Didn't I just see Sweet Pea a couple weeks ago, when you thought she might have the flu? And the month before that, when she bumped her nose on the dresser? We could have done the shots then, you know."

"I know that," she said. "You mentioned it — twice, if I remember. But I couldn't cancel the annual visit. Why, Sweet Pea's been looking forward to seeing you all day."

"Oh really." Garrett sounded about as enthusiastic as a teenager going in to get braces. Charlie, Garrett's Lab, stayed behind the reception desk, making himself scarce.

Sweet Pea barked again and jumped up, putting her paws on either side of the wall, sniffing at Catherine. Dottie came over and waved a biscuit at the dog, but Sweet Pea ignored her.

"Sweet Pea!" Miss Tanner pulled on the

dog's collar, but it had about as much effect as trying to hold back a team of horses. "That's not nice, baby."

Sweet Pea nosed forward, still snarfling at Catherine's hand. As if the dog sensed something strange, detected the feline side that lingered beneath her skin. Catherine had to remind herself that she was five foot five and taller than the dog right now. If Sweet Pea came back after sundown, now, that would be another story.

Garrett jerked at the leash again and led the whole entourage toward the exam room.

"She's been awfully mellow lately, Doc," Miss Tanner said.

Garrett raised an eyebrow. "Mellow?"

"And something's bothering her right back foot. I didn't see anything, but you know my vision. Let me tell you, young man, getting old isn't any fun. Damned eyes are the first thing to go."

"Oh, you're not old, Miss Tanner. You act younger than half the people I know," Garrett said as they entered the room. He gently pressed on the dog's hindquarters to encourage her to sit. Instead, the Doberman leapt to her feet, barking at dust motes in the air.

Miss Tanner turned and looked at

Catherine, her gaze narrowing. "Who's this? What happened to what's her name? The last girl who worked here?"

"This is Catherine. She's my new assistant." Garrett readied a few shots on a paper towel and flipped through Sweet Pea's chart.

"What are her qualifications? I can't have my Sweet Pea looked at by just anybody."

"She's here and she's not afraid of the dog. Right?" He glanced at Catherine over the top of the folder.

She took a breath, recentered herself and nodded. Sweet Pea was just a dog, albeit a very large one. Catherine knew how to handle a dog. She wasn't about to blow this, her first day on the job.

Garrett shrugged. "Good enough for me."

Miss Tanner harrumphed. Sweet Pea put in her two cents with lots of barks, the sound reverberating in the little room like a canine rock concert.

"Sweet Pea! Hush! I know you're excited to see him, but you have to let Doctor McAllister help you," Miss Tanner said.

Garrett laid the folder on the counter and came around, hands on hips, to stand in front of the dog. He looked at her. She looked at him. It reminded Catherine of a standoff she'd seen once outside a saloon in Dodge City.

Finally, Garrett bent down, put his hands under the dog's belly and tried to lift her onto the table. Sweet Pea, however, was having none of that. She scrambled out of his arms and backed up against the wall, nails clacking against the vinyl.

"Guess we'll leave her where she is."

Sweet Pea let out a chuff of victory.

Garrett knelt beside the dog and picked up her right rear paw. The dog turned and started barking in Garrett's face. Garrett, normally unruffled with any of the animals, seemed ready to lose his cool with the incorrigible dog.

I can handle you, Catherine thought. She'd done it before, but never as a human. But . . . if she tried hard enough, she might be able to summon up the energy she needed to connect with the dog.

Catherine took a deep breath, then moved forward and with both hands, cradled Sweet Pea's face. She knelt before the Doberman, in slow, gradual moves. The dog let out a short yip of a bark that lowered an instant later to a mere grumble in her throat. Catherine fixed her gaze on the dog's liquid brown eyes. "Shhh."

And just like that, Sweet Pea shushed.

She settled onto her haunches, complacent as a cow in a pasture.

Catherine could feel the hum of connection between her and the dog. It was faint, too faint to read anything more than Sweet Pea's general anxieties about everything. No wonder the dog barked all the time. She had all the courage of a ninety-pound knight about to undertake his first jousting match.

"Whatever you're doing, keep doing it," Garrett whispered across the dog's back. "I see a splinter in here." He reached for a set of tweezers on the counter above his head, then lay on the floor and set to work removing the sliver of wood.

"What'd you do? Slip her some drugs?" Miss Tanner leaned forward and squinted at Catherine. "I don't want my Sweet Pea doped up."

"She didn't drug your dog, Miss Tanner. She's good with animals."

Wow. Two compliments in one day. Dottie had been right — Garrett's bark was definitely worse than his bite. He was a lot like Sweet Pea in that respect.

She glanced at him. He had deftly removed the splinter and now was applying an antibiotic to the dog's foot and wrapping it with some gauze. All the while, he talked to Sweet Pea, the same sort of soft nothings she'd heard the night he'd picked her up.

He had the hard lines of a man's face, tempered by the scars that ran down his neck and disappeared beneath his collar. Somehow, the scars seemed to soften him, to add an edge of humanity she'd never seen in anyone she'd met in her centuries of wandering the Earth.

He was like her, in a way. This man who stayed on the fringe of humankind, separated by his appearance.

She watched his lips move as he murmured to the Doberman and thought of his lips on hers, drifting down her mouth, then trailing kisses along her neck —

Sweet Pea let out a booming bark and jerked her head backwards, out of Catherine's grasp. Before she could regain control of the dog, Sweet Pea had leapt to the side, crashing into a table of instruments and medicines. The connection had been severed between them and now, all hell was breaking loose.

Glass shattered, metal fell to the floor. Catherine scrambled to her feet and reached for the dog, kneeling before her and again locking gazes. It took a moment, but Sweet Pea came to a standstill, wagged her tail twice, then sat down.

"What happened?" Garrett asked. "You lose your concentration?"

"Something like that."

"Well, don't let it happen again." He worked his way through the dog's exam, checking feet and teeth, feeling her belly, then finally filling syringes and administering the rabies and distemper shots. A few minutes later, he rose and turned to wash his hands in the sink. "Sweet Pea's all set, Miss Tanner."

"And she's fine?"

"Yes, but you need to knock off the crullers with her. She's getting a little . . . portly."

"But my Sweet Pea loves her crullers, don't you, baby?" Miss Tanner leaned down and gave the Doberman a smack of a kiss on the head. Either the mention of doughnuts or the kiss grabbed Sweet Pea's attention and she jerked out of Catherine's grasp again, barking like the world was about to end and she needed to have her say first.

"You're all set," Garrett shouted above the din. "See you in a year."

Miss Tanner left, dragging the dog behind her. Sweet Pea tried for one last lunge at Catherine's hand, but ended up only getting air.

"Whew. Thank God that's over," Garrett

said when they'd finally left. The sound of barking grew more and more distant with each passing second. "Dottie always mails her the bill so we can get Sweet Pea out of here as soon as possible." He closed his eyes and leaned against the counter. "Ah . . . quiet."

"Well, I guess that's it. Thank you. It was rather fun." Catherine brushed the dog hair off her skirt and then washed her hands in the sink.

"You're not leaving."

"You told me I could."

"Well, I'm changing my mind." He cleared his throat. "You were right."

She paused and pivoted back. "Did you say what I thought you said? Did you just tell me I was right?"

"I'm giving you a compliment, not a confession. Why do you have to be so difficult?"

Catherine raised an eyebrow in response. "*I'm* difficult?"

"You're not implying I am, are you?"

She grinned. "If the shoe fits —"

He held up a finger and stopped her mid-sentence. "You're the one wearing someone else's shoes right now."

"Touché." Catherine chuckled. "You got me there."

A shadow of a smile crossed his face, as if he wanted to joke back, to take it a step further, but then he retreated into doctor mode again. All business. No humor. "You're a good assistant," he said. "And, well, I'd be crazy to let you go."

"Are you admitting I was right?" She pressed again, teasing him.

He scowled. "I'm offering you a job. Are you accepting it or not?"

She smiled, feeling the joy extend from her heart into the muscles in her face. This was the job she'd dreamed of all her life. She'd proven herself. Showed him — and herself — that she could do it. And now, here was her dream, coming true on a cold, sunny November afternoon in Indiana.

She only had this one chance before her life as a human disappeared forever. Oh, how great it would be to spend it here, working with the animals. Now all she needed was a quiet place to spend the last of her human days and to find the kittens and her life would be perfect.

"Yes. Absolutely *yes*." She put out her hand.

Garrett hesitated a fraction of a second before taking her palm with his own.

"You have yourself an assistant, Doctor

McAllister," she said. Heat curled between them, the same tie she'd felt before when she'd stumbled into his arms and kissed him.

When they shook, a surge of electricity told her the job came with a fringe addition she hadn't counted on — a searing attraction to Garrett.

With it came risks. Of losing her heart. Of being distracted from her goals for these last few days. And, most of all, of depending on someone else.

If there was one lesson Hezabeth had taught her, it was that risks only led to disaster.

Six days. That's all she had left. She had to remember that, not how wonderful his hand had felt in hers.

They worked their way through the rest of the morning's patients in quick order, falling into a sort of system. Catherine would calm the animal, as she had with Sweet Pea, and Garrett would do all the exams and shot-giving. Just as well — Catherine wasn't much on wanting to see the shots administered. She was much happier one-on-one with the animals than the needles.

More than once, she caught Garrett

glancing at her over a complacent Chihuahua or a purring Persian with surprise in his eyes. Then he'd dip his head and get back to work, all business again.

Every time he did that, her heart did this strange flutter-flip thing and her concentration deserted her like Napoleon's army after the defeat at Waterloo.

She was a little light-headed from a lack of food, that was all. Soon as she got something in her stomach, Garrett would stop making it roll over like the obedient Jack Russell terrier in front of her.

"All set," Garrett said. "Spike checks out just fine, don't ya?" He ruffled the terrier's fur, gave him a quick scratch behind the ears and released him into his owner's arms.

"That's my boy." The man, tall, lanky and the polar opposite of his short, wiry dog, paused. "Are you sure he's okay? It's just, lately, he's been a little . . . mopey."

Spike sighed and pressed his head closer to his owner. His eyes, though, went to Catherine, communicating the same message he'd sent earlier when she'd been holding him.

"I don't see anything medically wrong, Mr. Wright. He's a good dog. Did just fine with me." Garrett picked up Spike's chart and began making notations.

"He's lonely," Catherine interjected before she could stop herself.

Both men swiveled to look at her. "Lonely? How do you know that?"

She swallowed. "It's . . . it's a guess," she stammered. "You mentioned earlier that you live alone, and I figured he probably doesn't get out much with other dogs."

Mr. Wright pursed his lips and gave her a long, assessing look with clear blue eyes that didn't seem to miss anything. "You think my Spike is, ah, lacking in female companionship?"

"Not necessarily female," Catherine said. "Canine."

He considered that for a moment, then chucked Spike under the chin and stroked the dog's head. "I guess I have been spending too much time watching the world from my couch. Might do me and Spike some good to get out and see more of my neighborhood. My granddaughter Jenny's been bugging me to take Spike on walks. To stop being a hermit." He rubbed at the terrier's ears. "Time I listened to good advice, isn't it, boy?" Spike yipped in response, his tiny tail wagging like a vigorous white flag. Mr. Wright tipped his chin in Garrett's and Catherine's direction.

"Thanks, Doc. Thanks to you, too, Miss."

When he was gone, Garrett turned to Catherine. Something had transpired in this exam room, but he couldn't quite put his finger on what. He'd been feeling this odd tension between them all day and now, after her comments about Spike, he knew why. "What was that about?"

Catherine picked up the bottle of cleaner and sprayed the stainless steel table. "What do you mean?"

"That . . . that," he gestured for the words he didn't have, "that whole thing about reading Spike's mind. Telling Mr. Wright the dog was lonely."

"Just a guess, that's all." She'd turned away from him and seemed to be very busy scrubbing at the shiny surface.

"I don't buy that for a second."

Catherine froze and drew in a sharp breath. The air between them grew silent and still.

"I'm right, aren't I?"

"How could you have known?" Her voice was soft with surprise. She pivoted slowly, the rag hanging limp in her hands. "I — I didn't think it was obvious."

"Oh, it was obvious all right." He laid the folder on the opposite counter. How could a woman he'd met a few hours ago upset his carefully constructed life so easily? He'd worked for years to seal himself off, to stop feeling, stop remembering, stop connecting with anyone that didn't come with fur. He'd learned his lesson with Nicole years ago — women didn't want a man who looked like him. He'd become the friend they wanted to have, the shoulder they'd cry on, but not a man they'd date. Or take into their beds. Better to be alone, he'd realized, than to be a "friend."

And now, here Catherine was, asking questions, dropping hints. Making him think about things he'd rather not think about. He scowled. "That whole thing about hermits and loneliness and not getting out much."

Catherine blinked at him. *"Hermits?"*

"Was that some kind of hint?" He took a step forward, invading her space. Almost immediately, he regretted the action because it put him closer to her gray-green eyes and that insanely short black skirt. Her nearness only seemed to inflame him more, make his temper — and his temperature — rise. "That I need to get out more? Maybe get more than 'canine' companionship?"

Catherine Wyndham, the woman who

had appeared naked in his office that morning, opened her mouth and laughed like hell. "Is that what you thought?" She laughed some more, nearly bending in half. "That I was talking about you?"

"Well . . . well . . . yes," he sputtered. "You can stop laughing at me now."

She choked back the rest of her laughter. "I'm sorry. I'm not laughing at you. I'm really not. I just," she threw up her hands, "I just thought you meant something else, that's all. I really was talking about the dog." Her face sobered and her gaze zeroed in on his.

Garrett knew then why all the animals quieted the minute Catherine held them. She had a power in those eyes — mesmerizing, bewitching. He wanted nothing more than to stare into those eyes and forget everything in his past, everything in his present. To think only of her.

At that moment, nothing existed but Catherine. He thought of the kiss earlier, of the taste of her mouth against his, of the feel of her in his arms.

So many years. So lonely.

The thought came into his head again, echoing as if she'd had it, too. He held his hands against his side, clenching fists that wanted only to pull her to him and touch again. Connect again.

Feel again.

Her breath went in. Out. Her chest rose and fell under the hot pink shirt. He didn't move, didn't even know if his heart still beat.

"Each of us is lonely in our way." Her voice wrapped around him, as easily as her gaze had. "Do you feel it, too?"

He thought of the dark, empty bed that greeted him at the end of every day. How could she know about him? About his life?

It would be so easy to admit that to her. To this stranger who'd come out of nowhere and made him start to question the walls he'd built so well and for so long. But to do so would be crazy. Opening himself up to someone who hid her real identity, her past.

"It's the fault of the furniture manufacturers," he said instead. Humor was easier. Safer. "Too much comfort and the next thing you know, it's just you and the remote —"

She placed a finger on his lips and he stopped talking. "Don't. Don't joke. I couldn't bear it if you treated this like a joke. Don't you sometimes feel that way, too?" She paused for a breath, and it seemed every emotion she'd ever had pooled in her face. "Lonely?"

He opened his mouth to answer her, but the words wouldn't come. He didn't know her. Didn't want to know her or anyone else. Let people in and before you know it, they were asking questions, probing, feeling "sorry" for him. Better to keep that door shut. Locked.

"There's work to be done," he said. His lips moved against her finger, tasting the sweet softness of her skin. Inside, his body groaned, arguing with his sensibilities, screaming at him to shut the hell up and kiss her instead.

"There's always work to be done," she countered, moving her hand away from his mouth.

"My point exactly. I can't stand around lollygagging all day like I'm on some talk show." Even if he wanted to, he couldn't. Wouldn't. "I have things to do. Lots of things to do." Though he couldn't think of a single one.

She nodded and bit her lip. "Yeah. Important things, I'm sure."

When she turned away and went back to cleaning, he knew. He'd hurt her. And he couldn't undo it — not without opening that locked door.

God didn't make Eve from Adam's rib.

He took out half of Adam's brain by accident. Garrett vowed to steer clear of Catherine the rest of the day. Then maybe his stupidity wouldn't be so obvious.

The silence in the room weighed more than Sweet Pea on his chest.

He cleared his throat, but it didn't take away the heavy guilt. He racked his brain for something that could. "I bet you don't have a place to stay."

As far as apologies go, that probably wasn't his best.

She glanced up from the table. "I just arrived in town yesterday. I haven't had a chance to find anything yet."

"I might be insane for even offering this, but . . ." He turned and scribbled out an address on a slip of paper as he spoke. "My Aunt Mabel has this cottage on her property. Normally, I live there. But my aunt's been sick, so I'm staying with her in the main house for a few days. The cottage is just getting dusty. So use it if you want to." He handed the paper to her.

"Are you sure?"

"You don't have a place to stay, do you? You don't seem to have much money, either. I'm trying to be a nice guy here. So just let me do it."

She bit her lip, considering. "There's no

. . . strings attached to this offer, are there?"

"Strings?" It took him a second to figure out what she meant. That alone told him it had been too long since he'd dated. "Hell no. I told you, I'm just being a nice guy."

She raised an eyebrow. He figured he deserved that.

Garrett took a second piece of paper from the pad on the counter and scribbled out directions. "It's only a few blocks from here. It's not much, so don't expect the Taj Mahal or anything. And I'm not much of a housekeeper. Nor am I a decorator. It's just a place to sleep." Though he never did that there, either.

"Does it . . ." she bit her lip again, "does it have a white picket fence by any chance?" Her voice had gone soft, almost dreamy.

"Actually, yes, it does. It used to be the gardener's place when the home was part of an estate. Then most of the grounds were sold off to be a subdivision with a bunch of matching khaki-colored two stories. But the cottage does still have this little fence around it."

A smile spread across her face, wide and genuine. "And I can stay there for the next few days?"

"As long as you don't take the silver."

Now why did he say that? He didn't even own any silver. It had been going quite well, and then he had to throw that in there as if he were determined to sabotage anything friendly between them.

He'd done a damned good job of it, too. Her face hardened and she turned away, back to her cleaning. No germ would dare come near that table again when she was through with it. "Thank you," she said, curt and hurt.

There was a knock and Dottie poked her head in. "That's it for patients, until tomorrow."

"It's four already?" Garrett asked. Tuesday was his day to close early, in case he had surgeries scheduled. "No surgeries today?"

"Nope, not a one. And actually, it's not even quite three-thirty yet. You two made such a great team, we're way ahead of schedule. You did work through lunch because we had a lot of walk-ins, but everything was going so well, I didn't interrupt. I've never seen so many happy customers." Dottie winked. "Or so many happy patients."

"Good. Gives me more time to work with the shelter animals later." Garrett busied himself cleaning up from Spike's visit, tossing away used syringes and readying new equipment for the next patient.

"Doc?" Dottie said. *"Doc?"*

"Huh?"

"It's time to eat. We all skipped lunch, remember?"

"Oh, yeah." He waved at Dottie. "Go ahead and get yourself some lunch."

She gave him a frown. "I wasn't thinking about me." Dottie tilted her head toward Catherine, who had returned to scrubbing the exam table with disinfectant. The way she was going at the thing, he suspected she saw his reflection in the metal.

Her little black skirt swayed against her hips like a hula dancer. The short pink top rose up and down as she reached forward and around the table.

Damn. Why couldn't Tiffany have left behind better wardrobe selections? Any more of this and he'd lose his mind.

Garrett cleared his throat. "Miss Wyndham, you can go to lunch now."

She paused in her cleaning. "Oh, that's okay," she said, "I'll stay here and help with the animals. I'm not really hungry." The slight rumble coming from her abdomen belied her statement.

Behind Catherine's back, Dottie wiggled

93

her eyebrows and mimicked eating with one hand while pointing to Garrett and then to Catherine.

Garrett shook his head.

Dottie nodded.

Garrett shook his head again.

Dottie smiled sweetly at her boss, then turned away. "Catherine, the doc has a tradition of taking every new employee out to lunch on their first day."

Garrett shot a glare Dottie's way but she very purposely ignored him.

Catherine stopped cleaning and laid the cloth on the table. Her stomach rumbled again. "Really?"

"Oh, yes. And since today is your first day, and it's gone so well, I think you deserve it." Dottie entered the room, took the spray bottle out of Catherine's hands and laid it on the counter; then she took Garrett firmly by the elbow and led him over to where Catherine was standing. "Isn't that right, Doc?"

Catherine turned her gray-green gaze on him. Every coherent thought he'd ever had slid out of his brain. So much for his vow to steer clear. He'd just made an illegal U-turn.

"Yeah, it's a tradition," he found himself saying, even though he knew there was no such thing in his office. He'd never once taken an employee out to lunch. The extent of his socializing with the staff involved ordering in pizza on busy afternoons.

Out of the corner of his eye, he saw Dottie's smile of satisfaction.

Damn, he hated it when she was right.

Chapter Five

Five minutes later, he found himself seated across from Catherine in one of those chain restaurants that sported memorabilia on the walls in an attempt to blend kitsch with chic. Soft rock music drifted from the speakers, low enough to keep from being annoying.

He figured he could get in, eat fast and get back to the office without losing too much time or getting more personally involved. He was out of his element here, among the wannabe collectibles and 1980's hit music. And out of his element with Catherine — three feet away, so much closer than she'd been in the office.

A too-perky waitress who didn't seem old enough to serve drinks, never mind spell *tilapia* bounced up to their table in a red and white checked uniform. "I'm Missy, your server. Can I get you a drink to start you off?"

"Tea for me," Catherine said. "Do you have Earl Grey back in the kitchen?"

The waitress blinked. "I don't think he works here. But I can check."

"No, it's a kind of tea."

A muscle-bound busboy sauntered by and Missy's attention traveled with him for a few seconds. "Uhhuh," she said, scribbling on her pad. "Well, we don't have an Earl Grey here. Sorry." She turned to Garrett. "And for you?"

It was too early for whiskey, unfortunately. Garrett had a feeling alcohol would have been a much better choice for getting through this meal without losing his head — or worse, opening that door he'd vowed a few minutes ago to keep locked and sealed. "Coffee. Black. Nothing fancy."

"In a cup?"

"Uh, yeah, that would help."

The waitress, clearly a little ditzy and easily confused, nodded. "Good. That's the easiest way for me to serve it." Then she was gone.

Garrett looked at Catherine. Catherine looked at Garrett. Again, the invisible tether snaked between them. Each of them let out a little laugh.

She shook her head. "Have you eaten here before?"

"No." He shrugged. "I figured since it was a chain, it would be okay. Predictable, you know?"

"You don't have a favorite restaurant in Lawford?"

He picked up his menu and unfolded it. "I don't get out much."

"I thought you took all your employees out on their first days."

Memo to self: Fire Dottie.

"Well, this is different."

"How?"

"Not all my employees are like you." He cleared his throat and pretended to be absorbed in his menu before she could ask anything else, or he could let another comment like that slip past his lips. "Now, are we going to order or play twenty questions?"

Catherine pursed her lips and studied him for a second. Her stomach must have won the debate because she picked up the menu and began to look it over.

Garrett tried to study his but all he saw was Catherine. The list of burgers and club sandwiches got lost amid her blond hair and gray-green eyes, just a few feet away. He found himself peering over the top of the oversized laminated paper, watching her read, wondering what she was going to choose, if she preferred blue cheese over ranch, if she took her platters with fries or baked potato. If she liked her eggs sunny-side up or scrambled . . .

Whoa. That was going into morning-after territory. Down a road he shouldn't travel. Thinking thoughts that involved way more than a boss-employee lunch.

So much for keeping things from getting too personal.

"Here's your latte and iced tea," Missy said, depositing their drinks on the table with a small flourish.

"I ordered coffee," Garrett said.

Missy sighed and dropped her chin, giving him the look teachers gave dense students. "Latte *is* coffee."

"But it's not what I ordered. And that's not what she ordered, either," Garrett pointed toward the iced tea sitting in front of Catherine. "She asked for *hot* tea."

Missy waved her hands in the air, as if all this was way too confusing. "I can put the glass in the microwave if you want."

"That's not how you make hot tea," Garrett growled. "Now take these drinks and —"

Catherine laid a hand over his and his anger dissipated like an ice cube in boiling water. "I like my tea cold, too."

"Great!" Missy said. "Now everybody's happy." She gave them a little wave and flounced off toward the kitchen.

"Wait!" Garrett called. Missy pivoted back. "We'd like to order."

The waitress laughed. "Oh, yeah. I always forget that part." She took out her pad and pen, flipped to a blank page, then looked to Catherine.

"The tuna club on rye, please." Catherine withdrew her hand from Garrett's, as if she'd just realized she'd still been touching him.

He told himself he didn't feel disappointed. Not at all. That it hadn't been years since a woman had touched his scarred hands so easily, as if nothing about him was unusual in the least.

Like he was a man to be desired. A man she *wanted* to touch.

"Gotcha." Missy scribbled, then nodded at Garrett. "And for you?"

He'd forgotten to choose something. He picked the first thing his gaze landed on in the menu list. "The, ah, Buster Burger with fries."

"You got it." She clicked her pen, slipped it back into her pocket, then bounced away.

Keep it impersonal, he reminded himself. He'd try to behave like a normal human being out on a business lunch, a man out with a woman — platonically. Though it had been so long since he'd done anything like that, he wasn't quite sure what the behavior entailed.

Certainly, it did *not* include thinking about kissing or otherwise touching the woman across from him.

"After the drink debacle, I hate to see what Missy considers a hamburger." He took a sip of the latte. "This isn't entirely terrible, though."

Catherine laughed. "I had no idea lunch with you would be such an adventure."

"I'm a boring Indiana veterinarian. My life isn't much of an adventure at all."

Catherine dropped her chin into her hands, her eyes wide and bright. "You're so wrong. Today was . . . *amazing.* I can't imagine doing what you do all day, every day." She took in a breath, let it out. "It was wonderful."

She reminded him of himself from years ago, full of fire, passion for the work. How long had it been since he felt that way? When had the daily stresses and the worries about money mounted up and doused that fire?

Garrett knew the exact day when that

had happened. Truth be told, it didn't have a damned thing to do with bills. The power punch for his job had gone out of the day-to-day a long time ago.

But Catherine had it. In her eyes, her hand movements, her voice. Maybe Catherine could —

No, that was a crazy idea.

"Penny for your thoughts," she said. "Actually, I don't have a penny right now, so I'll have to write you an IOU."

He smiled — a small smile, but one all the same. "I'll take it out of your check." He drummed his fingers on the table for a few seconds. "I wasn't thinking about much. Just . . . Nah, it's a crazy idea."

"What is?"

The shelter wasn't getting the funding any other way. What did he have to lose by asking her? He'd thought he could do this on his own, but clearly he lacked the people skills. Hell, he lacked all people skills.

He sighed, then forged forward. "I have this meeting with the board members of the Lawford Community Foundation on Saturday. I've met with them before, trying to get funding for the shelter."

"And?" she prompted when he didn't continue.

He cleared his throat. "And it seems I

don't have a good way with people. I tend to get a little . . . grumpy when things don't go my way."

She quirked a smile at him. "Really? I'd never guess that about you." Her smile grew. "You're always so pleasant with me. Could make a girl swoon if she wasn't careful." She winked.

Was she flirting with him? No, that was impossible. And yet, his pulse quickened anyway. It had been years since a woman had flirted with him. Catherine's question from earlier haunted at the edges of his mind.

For a second he wanted to say yes, he knew what lonely was. He knew too damned well.

Instead, Garrett shook his head and got back to the task at hand. "In the past, my presentations haven't gone well. They've always turned me down. This is basically my last chance."

"And you're rather worried about it?"

"Very. You've seen the shelter. We need more room, more staff. If I had a full-time assistant, I could double the number of animals we cared for, make a real difference in finding them homes. Give them a chance at a life." He stopped himself and picked up his coffee. "Sorry. I get off on a rant sometimes."

Catherine, however, picked up his thread and ran further with it. "I think it all sounds wonderful. If you could care for more of these animals, it would make a big difference in the community, too. If you had enough space, you could offer teaching opportunities to children. Help them learn about caring for animals. They'd not only have a place where they could find their new pet, but also a great resource to learn how to care for it."

Garrett pointed at her. "*That* is exactly what I need."

"I agree. A space like that could —"

"Not the space. Well, yes, I need room, too, but I need *you*." Had he really just said that?

"You . . . you need me?"

"Here's your order!" Missy laid a plate of food between each of them. "The hamburger special and the tuna salad."

"Uh . . ." Catherine began, pointing toward the tuna atop lettuce and tomatoes in front of her. Then she threw up her hands and grinned at Garrett. "Never mind."

He grinned back. It felt so . . . odd to be smiling. How long had it been since he'd smiled? Over something going wrong? Normally, he would have raised a fuss, demanded to see the manager, made sure the

104

mistake was rectified. But today, with Catherine sitting across from him, smiling like it was a private joke between the two of them . . .

He didn't give a damn if Missy had brought him a live cow on the plate. "This looks delicious. Thank you."

Missy gave them a knowing, I-told-you-so nod, then be-bopped away, off to ruin someone else's meal.

Catherine speared some lettuce, but didn't eat. "Tell me more about the shelter, the foundation and what you're trying to achieve."

He pushed his plate forward and crossed his hands on the table. "There's a fund-raising dinner on Saturday with a meeting beforehand. The chairman's an old friend of mine. He agreed to give me one more chance at pitching the need for a bigger shelter. If I screw up this time, they'll probably ban me from showing my face there again."

"I don't understand how I figure into this."

"You . . ." he paused. *Oh hell, just say it.* "You have that passion I used to have. When I first started practicing veterinary medicine."

"Used to have?"

"Before the —" He shook his head. "Just before."

He could see she wanted to ask him about the sentence he'd left unfinished, but wisely didn't. Instead, she took a bite of her salad and munched. She swallowed, then pointed her fork his way. "You know, you're about as forthcoming as a mime."

"Sorry. I'm not a touchy-feely guy."

"I'd say not." She smiled again at him, tempering her words, layering them with another meaning. The double-entendre surprised him, teased at his senses. She *was* flirting. "Okay, one more time," she continued. "How *exactly* do I figure into this?"

"I want you to make the presentation for me."

"Me?" She sat back against her chair. "Why?"

"Because you're excited about this. You love animals." He paused, then tried on a smile again. It felt good. Damned good. "And you look better in a skirt than I do."

She cocked her head. "Was that a joke I just heard come out of Garrett McAllister's mouth?"

He grinned again. Too much of this and he'd be trying out to be a circus clown. "Hey, don't get used to it."

She laughed. "Too late. I already did." She twirled her fork, clearly considering his offer.

He pulled his plate toward him and took a few bites of his lunch, a ground beef and noodle mixture which admittedly, wasn't bad and probably a lot better for his heart than the cheeseburger and French fries he'd ordered. At least Missy had done his arteries a little good.

They ate for a while in silence, the comfortable kind of silence most people accumulated over years of knowing each other. He found it hard to believe they'd met a few hours ago. It felt as if they already knew each other or had met before. Another time, another place.

Missy came back and fluttered a white piece of paper at them. "Time to pay," she said, laying the bill on the table. "I hope you liked the service because I could really use the tip. I'm going to college and, man, is it expensive to get smart!" She flounced away, sending a wave over her shoulder.

Garrett chuckled and withdrew an extra ten from his wallet. "I think it's in our best interests to contribute generously to the Missy college fund."

Catherine smiled at him. "You're a good man."

Some teen idol sang about a broken heart on the sound system. In the kitchen, someone was shouting about a mistake. At the table beside them, a group of people were laughing at a punch line.

But all Garrett heard was the same four words over and over again. *You're a good man.*

Something long dead began to flutter to life inside his chest.

"Just for tipping generously?" he said. "Even Donald Trump does that."

"But I'm not having lunch with Donald Trump right now, am I?"

His right hand was on the table, inches from hers. What would she do if he reached forward right now and took hers with his own? "Would you rather be eating with him?"

"You mean, instead of you?"

She'd finished her salad and now pushed the plate to the side of the table. Her lips curved upward into a smile that warmed him from the inside out. Again, he wondered if he was reading her right. Was this friendly interest . . . or more? Everything within him wanted more.

Much more.

"I've eaten with princes and with paupers," Catherine said. "And to be honest,

I've had very few meals as enjoyable as this one."

"I'm glad the salad —"

"It wasn't the salad that I enjoyed," she said. She opened her mouth, as if she wanted to say something else, then stopped herself with a little mental shake. "I . . . I want to hear more about the foundation and the meeting on Saturday. But first, tell me why you became a vet," she said.

The shift in subject came as a surprise and it took him a second to remember their earlier conversation. Half his brain was still thinking about pursuing that intangible something more. "What's that have to do with helping me get the grant?"

She grinned. "I don't give my help to just anyone, you know. I want to be sure you're worthy of me putting on a dress and heels."

"Depends on how high the heels are going to be." Damn. Now *he* was flirting with her.

Her eyes were bright, her lashes lowered enough to tease him. "High enough," she said in a deep, throaty voice. "Believe me."

That husky little statement had now sent his libido spiraling into new territory.

"Uh . . ." he said, because he couldn't think of anything better and because his brain had dissolved into oatmeal, "what was the question again?"

The wind whipped around Catherine, nipping at her bare legs. The short skirt and thin coat did almost nothing to block the early winter temperatures. Luckily, she'd ditched the high heels after a second scavenger hunt in the storage room netted a pair of Tiffany's gold sparkle flats. But the rest of her was still clad in clothes that could use a lot more fabric. "I don't think it was this cold out when we walked down to the restaurant." She rubbed at her arms and shivered.

"November in Indiana isn't so bad." Garrett slipped off his overcoat and draped it over her shoulders.

The long wool coat smelled like Garrett, warm and woodsy. She should have refused it. She was a woman who took care of herself. She'd been cold before and she'd lived through it.

The coat was warm and soft. She'd be a fool to refuse it. She drew it tight and close, snuggling into the wool.

Almost like she was in his arms.

Now that was a crazy thought. The type that only led to trouble. She had her life planned out — find a quiet little house to live out the rest of her human days. She only had a few of those left and she wanted to spend them in a traditional, quiet environment pretending she'd lived the one life she'd been denied — the one with the white picket fence. That way she could have her dream and not have to find a man who would do the impossible, love her as a human *and* a cat. That's what she was supposed to be focused on and yet, all through lunch, the only thing she'd thought about had been Garrett. She'd flirted with him. Acted interested. But she wasn't.

Not one bit.

They had no future. After Saturday night, her existence as a woman would end. As a cat she was independent, uninvolved. Unemotional. Life, she'd found, was much safer that way. No broken hearts, no disappointments, no risks.

Until Saturday, it would be best to stay away from any further involvement with Garrett McAllister.

That would be easy — if only his coat didn't feel and smell so good. Like he had, that first night.

"You won't like it here in January and February, though," he said as they walked. He barely seemed bothered by the cold. "And by March, it'll seem like winter is never going to end."

"It's a beautiful place," she said, avoiding the subject of whether she'd be here a season, or even a month, from now. And it was. This part of downtown Lawford was called the historic district, she saw from the signs on the lampposts. Quaint brick and stone storefronts with bright striped awnings lined the sidewalks. Matching brick had been laid along the edge of the concrete sidewalks, keeping the old feel. Twin round globes hung from each side of the tall black wrought-iron lampposts. Planters of fall flowers ringed the posts, providing a wash of color against the dark surface.

"It's a nice town. A little too Mayberry-ish for most people, but nice," Garrett said.

"Mayberry?" she asked.

"You know, *The Andy Griffith Show*? Back when TV was black-and-white and people lived in perfect little houses with two parents, two kids and a dog?"

"I don't remember that show, but I do remember when television became color. It was amazing. I was walking by a store in New York City and there was this screen with all these colors, like a box full of rainbows." She shook her head. "I never really

112

watched television before that, but you started seeing TVs everywhere a few years later."

"The first color TV ever made was manufactured in Indiana because the RCA plant was here," Garrett said.

"Really? What a coincidence."

"Yeah, but that was in *1954*." He stopped and eyed her. "You're not that old. How could you have been around for that?"

Oh no. She'd done it again. Lost track of her story and said too much. The years sometimes blended together and she forgot that she was supposed to be twenty-five, not two hundred and twenty-five. "Ummm . . . well . . . my parents didn't allow television in the house and I didn't really see one until I was older and for me, it was like they'd, ah, just been invented."

"Uh-huh."

He clearly didn't buy it.

"What a gorgeous building!" She pointed to the first place she saw. It could have been a cardboard box for all she cared, as long as it helped her change the subject. "What is it?"

"The courthouse. Right next to the sheriff's office."

She heard the *hint, hint* in his voice. "Oh. Well, it's pretty."

"Looks nicer on the outside than it does from the inside."

Okay. Another subject is definitely in order.

"You never answered my question," she said. "What made you decide you wanted to be a vet?"

He smiled and she knew she'd finally latched onto the right topic. "Charlie."

"The same Charlie you brought to work today?"

They stopped at a crosswalk. When the light changed, Garrett placed a warm, comforting hand against the small of Catherine's back, a natural gentlemanly gesture she was sure he didn't realize he'd made, and guided her as they crossed the street.

"No, my first Charlie. A Labrador my parents gave me when I was seven. He was a hell of a dog, the original Charlie. I tortured the poor thing, I think, 'treating' him. He broke a leg chasing after a car and when I saw how the vet took care of him, I was hooked. Charlie came right through it and was ready to play sooner than anyone had expected. But don't let on to the current Charlie that he has a predecessor to live up to." They'd reached the other side of the street and he paused, lowering his voice to a whisper that brushed against her ear and sent a little of his warmth down her neck. "He's got a fragile ego."

"Your dog doesn't seem to do much but sleep. I'm not sure he has an ego."

Garrett chuckled. "He's getting old. All he wants to do is hang out wherever I am."

Catherine trailed a finger along the sill of a storefront. "It must have been nice."

"What must have been nice?"

"To have a dog as a kid. A pet. I never had one. Well, not one that was really mine."

"I thought most kids had something, even if it was a caterpillar they kept in a box in their room."

They had rounded the corner that ended the historic area of downtown and brought them to a little oasis of quiet. The late afternoon sun was brighter here, making the small park that ran behind Main Street warm and bright. Garrett gestured toward the park and Catherine nodded. They walked down the paved path, skirting the shaped shrubbery and fading mums that lined the edge of the walkway.

Garrett didn't want to go back to the office yet. Despite the temperature, he wanted to stay here, outdoors with Catherine. Few people were about, making it seem as if they were alone. He enjoyed her company, not just because she was a beautiful woman, but because they had so much in common. He had never met a woman whom he could relate to, who understood the way he thought and the things that were important to him.

She paused beside an elm and leaned against the tree. "I didn't grow up like most kids. My parents were . . ." her voice trailed off. "Well, I guess you would have considered them wealthy."

He heard the words "would have" and thought of probing, but didn't. Were her parents dead? Estranged from her? Or just in another place? "All antiques and no room for fur?"

"Something like that." She took in a breath and her gaze focused on something far beyond Garrett. He got the feeling she was looking years into the past. Grasping at memories from decades ago. That was impossible. She wasn't that old — in her mid-twenties, for sure — and her childhood wasn't that far behind her. And yet . . .

"When I could," she began quietly, her hand tracing along the bark of the tree, "I'd escape the French lessons and endless embroidery and get out of the house. Sometimes, there'd be a stray cat in the stables where they kept the horses and if I was very lucky, there'd be kittens. But they weren't very tame, not living like that. And the stable master didn't like having me underfoot. He considered a girl bad luck in the stables."

Stables. Horses. Stable masters. A life so foreign from his own, growing up in a three-bedroom ranch on a sunny side street in Lawford. There hadn't been much money, but there had been a warmth about his childhood, a mother who encouraged him to explore and endured his passion for bringing home strays. His father hadn't always been so happy to see yet another pet on the doorstep, but neither of Garrett's parents had ever really told him no. They'd recognized his love for animals early on and encouraged it, gently guiding him in his educational choices, paying for him to attend the best veterinary college in the country. Allowing him the time to work with Doc West and then cheering when he opened his own practice. Even from their retirement home in Florida, his parents remained his biggest supporters.

For the first time in a long time, Garrett realized he was a lucky man. "Why didn't you get a dog when you moved out on your own?"

"Oh, I wanted one." She swung away from the tree and crossed to a bench. She settled on it and slid over to make room for him. "It's just . . . I'm never in one place for very long."

He hesitated. The question hung in the air between them for several seconds before he finally asked it. "Why?"

She didn't answer. She picked up a leaf from the ground and began tearing it into tiny pieces. Behind her, the sun began to descend behind the trees, casting its last long bright rays of the day.

"Why do you move so much?" he asked again, his voice softer this time. He was pushing past the boundary he'd put in place this morning — the one that said Personal: Don't Cross — but he wanted to know, needed to know. "Catherine, what are you running from?"

She shook her head. "You don't understand. It's not all black-and-white for me. I can't just settle down and live like ordinary people."

He'd already opened the door. Might as well enter the room. "Why not?"

She gave him a small, sad smile. "You'd never believe me if I told you."

Tell me, he wanted to say. *Tell me everything. Tell me why you look like you're about to cry. Tell me why you shut me out when I start to get close. Tell me why I care so much about someone who seems so different . . . and yet so much like me.*

But he didn't say any of that.

Instead, he did what a man did best. Changed the subject. "Well, Saturday night you can help hundreds of kids get pets. Down the road, anyway." He smiled. "I'm not planning on expanding too much yet."

She tossed the rest of the leaf to the ground. "The meeting is Saturday . . . night?"

"Yes. There's a cocktail thing first, but the main event is at six."

"Six? That's too late. It's after sun—" she cut herself off, shook her head. "I can't go."

"What? Why not?"

She pushed at a pile of leaves with her toe. "I just can't."

"You have something else to do Saturday night?"

"Please don't press me on this, Garrett." It was the first time she'd used his given name and if it had been in any other circumstance but her turning him down for the most important thing in his life, he might have allowed himself a momentary twinge of joy.

"I don't understand why you won't do this."

"It's personal. I can't tell you any more than that." He let out a gust and got to his feet. "You tell me you want to help the animals. You're excited about the shelter making a real difference with more funding. Now here's your chance to help make that happen and all of a sudden *you can't?*"

She hung her head and the last rays of sun bounced glints off her golden hair. When she looked up at him again, her gray-green glistened with tears.

Maybe it was all an act. Maybe she was a con artist looking for a few dollars and a place to stay before she moved on to the next place. Maybe she didn't really care.

And maybe he shouldn't care either.

But he did.

He'd cared from the first second she'd shown up in his office with nothing to her name but an unbelievable story and a clear need for someone to take care of her.

"I'm sorry, Garrett," she said, her voice a hoarse, strangled whisper. "Please understand." She glanced at the sky, then back at him. She shrugged off his coat and pressed it into his hands. "I can't stay any longer. I have to go."

"Catherine —" he reached out and grasped one of her hands. "Don't go. Not yet. We had a deal, remember?" He gave her one of his new and improved grins. "I'll help you, after you help me?"

The sun was just disappearing beneath the horizon. Catherine winced as if she were in pain and yanked her hand out of his. "I have to go. Thank you for lunch." She hesitated for a fraction of a second, then placed a quick kiss on his cheek. "Thank you for a wonderful day, too."

Then she let out a gasp and wheeled away before he could stop her. She broke into a run, kicking off Dorene's shoes as she went, heading straight for the woods.

"Catherine, wait!" He yelled, trying to follow, but she dodged into the trees, vanishing into the woods like a sprite. "Are you all right? Where are you going?"

She didn't stop. She didn't answer. In a flash, she was gone.

For the second time that day, Catherine Wyndham had left him holding his coat, mouth agape and confused as hell.

Chapter Six

Garrett stumbled out of bed at six the next morning and headed for the kitchen, looking for coffee. Not conversation.

He got both. Aunt Mabel sipped from a china cup at her small oak table, already dressed in a sweater and slacks. As usual, she'd had a head start on the day. Her dark brown hair was in a tight bun, her bright pink lipstick applied, the morning paper opened and half-read beside her.

A steaming mug of coffee sat in front of Garrett's customary seat. He took a big gulp, then eased into the chair. He held up the mug to her, a toast of thanks. "*This* is why you are my favorite aunt."

"I'm your only aunt," she said, turning to the Living section.

He grinned. "If I had others to choose between, you'd still be my favorite."

"Because we're related by blood?"

Garrett took a second sip. The caffeine

started to shake that groggy feeling from his mind. He'd spent too many hours tossing and turning last night. Thinking about Catherine. If he'd been smart, he would have dreamed her right out of his system. "No. Because you work miracles with coffee grinds."

"You really know how to flatter a woman." She chuckled. "By the way, did you get another cat?"

"Another cat?"

Aunt Mabel closed the paper, then picked up a skirt from the basket by the table. She started in where she'd left off the night before, hemming it for one of her dressmaking customers. "A pale orange tabby. Cute little thing."

Garrett's ears perked up. It couldn't possibly be the same cat. And yet, he lived only a few blocks from the office, so it wasn't improbable. "Where did you see her?"

"Outside, pawing at the door of the cottage like she was trying to get in. I think she was looking for a warm place to sleep."

"She's not mine. But she sounds like she might be the stray that got loose at my office the other day."

Aunt Mabel laid down her sewing and started to rise. "Do you want some eggs?"

"Yes I do, but no, I don't want you to make them for me." Garrett got to his feet. "You should be resting, not hemming skirts or making me eggs."

"I'm fine. Have been for three days now. The doctor gave me a clean bill of health on Tuesday." She reached out and touched his arm as he went by. "Why won't you?"

"You're seventy-four, Aunt Mabel. You need someone to take care of you."

"Seventy-four is not dead, you know. I'm perfectly capable of taking care of myself. You didn't need to move in here."

"You were sick. I wanted to be here in case something happened."

Aunt Mabel gave his arm a squeeze. "And I love you for it, Garrett. You're my favorite nephew," she gave him a teasing grin, "but you have one bad habit."

"I snore too loud?"

"You think you have to rescue everyone and everything you come across." She let go of his arm and waved toward the yard. "You should go back to your own house and find your own life. Get married, settle down."

Garrett pulled open the refrigerator, rummaged around until he came up with a dozen eggs, and placed the cardboard carton on the counter. "I can't. Go back to the cottage, I mean."

"Why not?"

He started looking for the bacon. "I met this woman —"

"Wonderful!"

He jerked back so fast, his head nearly collided with the refrigerator shelf. "No, no, I didn't mean like that." In an instant, Aunt Mabel would be measuring him for a tux. "She's working for me and needed a place to stay for a few days." Back in the fridge he went, withdrawing with the bacon in one hand, butter in the other. "So I offered her the cottage."

"Is she there now?"

"I doubt it. I forgot to give her the key before she . . . she left yesterday." *Before she dashed into the woods like a lunatic.*

He decided not to share that part of the story with his aunt.

Aunt Mabel crossed to the stove, moved a cast iron skillet onto the front burner and lit the gas flame. "What is she? Another stray you rescued?"

"It's not like that at all. It's . . . complicated."

She arched a brow his way. "Uh-huh."

"How do you want your eggs?"

His aunt didn't fall for the change of subject. She moved to the sink, washed her hands and glanced out over the yard. "I think you need a woman. You don't even have curtains on your windows, for Pete's sake. I should get out some fabric and —" She paused. "Well, I'll be."

"What?"

"Seems your houseguest did find her way home last night."

"The cat?"

"If *she's* a cat, then I really need new glasses." Aunt Mabel pointed out the window.

I'll be damned.

Catherine Wyndham sat in the old wooden rocker on his tiny front porch, her white-sock-clad feet propped on the railing. She held a mug between her hands. Of coffee, he presumed, since he didn't have any tea. The risen sun cast a golden hue over her, like a natural halo.

It would have been a cliché to call her an angel, but seeing her cast such a sense of peace over his heart, he had no doubt she'd been a gift from the gods. Had she really only come into his life a couple days ago?

How everything had changed in such a short time.

His heart skipped a beat. Then another. "I have to go," Garrett said. "Go, ah, talk to her."

"What about the eggs?"

He blinked. "Eggs?"

Aunt Mabel laughed. "Never mind." She shooed him toward the door. "Go on. Get out of here. Find yourself some love in the garden."

"Aunt Mabel —"

"Don't argue with me. I'm your favorite aunt, remember?"

Garrett grabbed a jacket and a pair of boots out of the mudroom by the back door and clomped his way through the damp grass to the cottage.

His pace slowed. Catherine, framed by the blooming chrysanthemums and the roses that trailed up the fence, seemed to have been transported in from another era. She had on a soft blue sweatsuit that blended with the scenery and offset her golden hair and gray-green eyes.

If he'd been an artist, he would have captured the scene on canvas. Maybe if he had her in a frame, instead of in his mind all the time, he could get some sleep.

"What are you doing here?"

Catherine popped forward in her seat. Her feet landed on the wooden floor with a soft plop. "Good morning to you, too. If I remember right, you gave me permission to stay here."

"I did. I just didn't give you a key."

She bit her lip. "I found another way in. I, ah —" She took a sip of coffee, stalling. He stared at her, waiting.

"The door was locked," he said. "I know because I locked it from the outside and I carry the key in my pocket. The windows are also locked, especially with the weather turning colder. So, tell me, how did you get in?"

"I, ah . . ."

"Well?"

"I went in through the, ah, chimney." The words came out in a cough-mumble.

He glanced at the thin brick chimney atop the little house. Then back at her. "The chimney? That's impossible."

She gave him a very bright grin that dared him to disagree. "Apparently not for me."

He considered the smokestack again, then shook his head. Maybe she was thinner than he thought. Either way, she was here, and relief coursed through him at knowing she was safe. He stood there, his boots making deep impressions in the lawn, and realized he hadn't a valid excuse for being out there. Her gaze, so direct and so disarming, had him wanting to retreat to Aunt Mabel's for more coffee.

"Well." He shifted from foot to foot. "I just wanted to see how you were. Be sure you're on time for work." He turned and clomped away, his boots squishing in the damp grass.

"Why do you insist on giving me such a hard time?" She'd caught up to him, running alongside in her socks.

"Your feet are going to get soaked. You should go get some shoes on."

"Right now, it's more important that I talk to you."

"See me at work." He started off again.

She followed right along. "It's difficult to talk there. I'd rather —"

He scooped her up into his arms before she could finish the sentence. "If you're going to be difficult, then I'll carry you. That way, I won't be responsible for you catching the flu."

"I am not some damsel in distress who needs you to rescue me every time I turn around."

"Oh yeah?"

"Yeah." But she didn't move out of his arms. He took that to mean he was right.

Every inch where she connected with him simmered with heat, as if November had turned to August in the space between their bodies. The blue fleece of her sweatsuit brushed against his arms, soft as velvet. He kept his eyes straight ahead, on the back porch of Aunt Mabel's house. Focused on anything but her mouth and how easy it would be to kiss her again.

The hundred-yard journey ended too quickly. He reached the porch and lowered her to the top step. "There."

She brushed at invisible lint on her pants. "Thank you."

"If you want to come in, we can have some breakfast and talk. My Aunt Mabel is there, but she's probably busy at her sewing machine. She's a seamstress," he added as explanation. "Retirement is not a word in her vocabulary."

He opened the door and ushered her in before him. Charlie scrambled to his feet and padded over to greet Catherine. "Hey, Charlie," she said, ruffling the dog's ears. The Lab pressed himself against Catherine like a long-lost friend.

The scent of crisp bacon and scrambled eggs caught his attention. He knew what had been happening in his absence.

Aunt Mabel, matchmaker.

Two plates sat on the kitchen table. Not just ordinary plates either, but two of her best china ones, complete with silver forks and dainty cloth napkins. Matching rose-patterned cups sat in saucers flanking each place setting, steam rising from the fresh coffee inside them. The radio in the living room had been tuned to the soft classics station. Frank Sinatra's "Fly Me to the Moon" provided an undercurrent for Aunt Mabel's romantic tableau.

"You did all this for me?" Catherine said.

For a second, he considered taking the credit, just to see her smile. There'd be repercussions to that, though. She'd think he was interested. And he most definitely wasn't. Not anymore. Not really. "No. I had nothing to do with it."

She surveyed the table again. "Let me guess. Aunt Mabel?"

From the other room, a sewing machine began to whir. "I doubt it was the Tooth Fairy."

Catherine smiled. "She must be one heck of an aunt."

"She is. Except when she gets an idea in her head, because then there's no stopping her." He raised one of the china cups as evidence, and took a sip. "But she can cook, and she makes the best coffee I've ever tasted."

"Better than Missy?"

The shared memory hit him in the solar plexus. It shouldn't have. It was a silly little moment in his life. A cup of coffee and the wrong cup at that.

And yet, one latte and he'd left the restaurant yesterday afternoon with hope in his heart. Feeling recharged, happier than he had in years. The feeling had lasted all of five minutes.

When she'd taken off into the woods, he'd told himself he was through helping her. He'd figured the last he'd see of Catherine Wyndham would be the short black skirt blending into the trees.

But he'd been wrong.

She stood in his aunt's kitchen, her skin gilded with sunlight, her smile wide and genuine, and he knew he was fooling himself if he thought he could forget about her.

Harry Connick, Jr. began to croon "It Had to Be You." Catherine hummed along with the tune, her hips swaying a bit. The melody tingled up his spine.

Before he could think about what he was doing, Garrett laid down the cup, then stepped forward and swooped Catherine into his arms. Wrapping one arm around her waist and grabbing her hand with his free one, he began to dance her around the sunny yellow kitchen.

"What are you doing?" Her voice filled with soft wonder.

"Sweeping you off your feet." Her body fit against his with precision, melding into all the right places. He'd danced with women before, but never had it felt like this.

They stepped to the right, swaying with the big band rhythm. The tinkling of the piano keys formed a soft undertow of sound as they stepped to the right, slid, then stepped back, slid, stepped left, slid and then moved forward in a perfectly synchronized box step.

They glided across the pale yellow vinyl floor, as if they were skating on ice. "You are good at this," she said.

"My mother insisted on lessons." He grinned. "She sold me on it by saying it was a good way to meet girls."

Her answering smile zinged through him louder than the bleat of the trumpets. "It is."

"You're not so bad yourself."

"Too many waltzes." She laughed. "My mother insisted, too."

"Here's to *very* wise mothers." Garrett bent his knee and dipped Catherine back, then scooped her into his arms again and spun her to the right.

She laughed. "I've never had this much fun dancing."

"Maybe you had the wrong partner."

Catherine's gaze locked with his, the smile replaced with something far more serious. The music went bump-bump-bump. His heart ran twice that rate. "I think that's exactly it," she said quietly.

Harry paused in singing and the band trilled. Garrett grinned and gave Catherine another little spin. She tossed back her head and laughed again, her hair swinging in a wild golden arc. Then his arm went around her waist again, hauling her to him and stepping to the right. She moved easily in his arms, as if she had danced with him a hundred times before.

As if they were meant to be partners.

"You are incredible," she said between breaths. "You surprise me all the time."

"Hmmm . . . I beg to differ." He pressed her palm with his and she took a step back, reading the body language. "You're the one who —"

"This must be a heck of a lot easier than wrestling with German shepherds all day."

Garrett broke away from Catherine and pivoted toward the back door. His good friend Jake Aiken stood in the doorway, grinning like a fool. And with all the timing of one.

"What brings you by so early?" Garrett tried to keep his voice neutral.

"You asked me by, remember?" Jake waved his hands in a circle. "Sort of a strategy meeting for Saturday?"

"Sorry, it slipped my mind." Ever since Catherine had walked into his life, his brain had gone on vacation.

Jake's grin widened. "I can see why." He stepped forward and put out his hand. "Since my friend here seems to have a total lack of social graces, I'll introduce myself. Jake Aiken."

Catherine and he shook. "Catherine Wyndham. Pleased to meet you."

"If I'm interrupting something —" Jake began.

"No, no. You're not interrupting at all. We were just about to have something to eat." Garrett gestured to the table. "Do you want some coffee? Eggs?"

"I ate, thanks." Jake took a seat at the table, draping his jacket over the back of the seat. "You already have my vote, you know. No need to drag out the china to butter me up."

"That wasn't for you. It was —" Garrett cut himself off. "Do you want some coffee or not?"

Jake gave the china a dubious glance. "If you can give it to me in a cup that won't break if I blow on it, yeah."

While Garrett poured coffee into a mug for Jake, Catherine edged toward the door. Every time she was near Garrett, she risked too much. She forgot herself and the curse. Yesterday had been too close of a call, with the transformation coming an instant after she'd reached the woods. And then, dancing with him, she'd felt . . . human, as if she didn't have a care in the world. As if Saturday night wasn't going to come.

Last night, sleep had eluded her as much as the kittens. She'd tried to track them, but was too far from where she'd last caught their scent. Finally, she'd given up and gone to the cottage, seeking the one type of home she'd never had — a traditional, quiet little space filled with flowers and warmth.

And finding instead reminders of Garrett everywhere. His shirt, the cuffs still folded back, left on the back of a recliner. His cologne on the blue terry robe on the back of the bathroom door. A pair of slippers by the bed, worn and comfortable as an afghan. He was in every inch of the cottage.

And even on the fresh coat of paint of the white picket fence, damn him.

She couldn't put him from her mind, nor

from her life. She'd snuck out at dawn, snagging fresh clothes from a nearby laundry line, and then returned to the cottage, telling herself she was there to absorb the atmosphere.

And hoping like heck Garrett would be part of the view.

It was too dangerous to be near him. She had a sneaking suspicion if she didn't leave now, she might never leave because her emotions would get all tangled up with her resolve.

"I can catch you at the office later," Catherine said, her hand on the knob.

"No. Stay." Garrett pulled her hand away and led her to the table. "Eat. Jake will act like a gentleman."

"Only if Casanova here does." His friend gave him another grin.

Garrett sent him a glare, which Jake ignored. He pulled out a seat for Catherine. She wavered, and half turned away, but then Garrett caught her eye with his own brown gaze and smiled at her. It sparked the same sense of belonging, of home, as it had that first night. Before she could rethink her decision, she took the offered seat.

Garrett settled into the opposite chair. "Okay. Tell me again the plan for Saturday."

"Well, there are cocktails at four-thirty.

Dinner is at five. Then the chairman," he placed a hand on his chest, "will make a long-winded and ridiculously boring speech while the alcohol kicks in. Once everyone is properly inebriated, I'll let you take the floor. Try to be pleasant and maybe you'll get your funding this year."

Garrett scowled. "I am pleasant."

"And porcupines make good pets, too." Jake leaned toward Catherine. "You seem to know how to make this guy smile. Think you can bring out his best side on Saturday?"

"Actually —" Garrett began.

Catherine shook her head. "I can't. I have another . . . obligation that night."

"She's a better presenter than I am," Garrett went on, overriding her objection. "I think she has a better shot at convincing the board than I ever would."

"Garrett, I told you I didn't think I could be there." There had to be another way she could help him. His shelter was important to him, and to her, especially now that she had worked there. But there was no way she could be there in person to plead his case.

Not on Saturday night. *The* last night. She was terrified that she'd be there, in front of all those people, making an impassioned plea to save the animals . . . and then transform into one herself.

She couldn't take that risk.

Jake stole a strip of bacon from Garrett's plate and took a bite. "Why not?"

Catherine shook her head. "I have something else to do."

"Garrett, would you mind helping me move this serger?" Aunt Mabel called from another room.

He got to his feet. "I'll be back." He cast a look at Jake. "She's damned good with animals and she cares about them like no one I've ever met before. I can't get her to say yes; maybe you can change her mind."

When he was gone, Catherine decided to eat as fast as possible and get out of there before Garrett tried again to rope her into speaking on behalf of the shelter Saturday night. If only the foundation were meeting during the daylight hours, then maybe she could help him without taking such a monumental chance.

And now for our next speaker, Garfield the cat.

Nope, it would never work. She simply couldn't do it.

Jake waved his pilfered bacon her way. "Listen, between you and me, Garrett is a great guy. He'd throw himself in front of a runaway truck for the people he loves. I've known him since I was four years old and I've never had a better friend. But . . ." He cast a look down the hall where Garrett had gone, then lowered his voice and leaned closer. "If you've known him longer than five minutes, then you know he's not as comfortable with people as he is with furballs."

Catherine smiled. "He's a good man."

"I never said he wasn't." Jake took a bite, crunched for a minute, then spoke again. "If you're nervous about making a presentation, then just be there for him. You don't even have to talk. He needs someone besides me in his corner against that stuffy old board."

"I want to help him, I really do. I . . . I can't."

Jake took a sip of coffee, then got to his feet. "I've only known you for thirty seconds, but I'll tell you something. *You are good for Garrett.* And by the look on your face when he was dancing with you, he's good for you, too. Whatever it is you have going on Saturday night, change it." He swung his coat off the back of the chair and slipped it on. "I don't know you and I don't know your story, but I do know him. If you care about him at all, you'll be there."

Chapter Seven

Catherine only had four days left to keep screwing up as a human. Thank God. Life would be a lot easier as a full-time feline. She'd be independent, uninvolved. There'd be no human feelings to worry about. No stupid mistakes to rectify.

No Garrett McAllister on her mind every minute of the day.

If that were so, the little voice in her head asked, then why had she come to work this morning? She'd left Aunt Mabel's house right after Jake did, taking the coward's way out. She'd intended to go back to the cottage and hole up there until Saturday night.

Forget dancing in the kitchen. Forget the lunch out with him. Forget the way he made her laugh, the way his smiles caused this odd tickle deep in her gut.

She hesitated outside the door to the building, clutching the coat she'd borrowed from a Goodwill bin. Oh, how she loved this place and loved the job she had. If only it didn't come with so many strings.

Catherine bit her lip, then, before she could change her mind, opened the door and stepped into chaos. The scene in the reception area reminded her of the fashion week she'd once attended in Milan, when the claws came out and the niceties got left at home. A bichon frise was telling off a Siamese cat, while a pair of mahogany setters chased each other around the chairs in the lounge. The cacophony of pets created the world's worst orchestra.

A small thin girl with messy blond braids stood in the middle of it all. She held no animal in her arms, yet her shoulders hunched around her, as if she had just released her favorite pet. Dottie and Garrett were busy trying to help the owners corral the worst of the four-legged offenders and line up the first appointments. Neither noticed the dejected child amid the zoo.

Catherine crossed to her, touching her lightly on the shoulder of her navy wool coat. "Can I help you?"

When she turned, her cornflower-blue eyes welled up, but didn't spill over. She was small and thin for her age — which Catherine estimated to be about ten — but her eyes made her seem older. "I'm looking for my cat."

"I'm sure she's here somewhere." Catherine peered around the furniture. "The dogs probably scared her."

The girl shook her head and pointed a thumb toward the door. "She's out there somewhere. With her babies."

"Is she lost?"

The girl nodded. "I lost her. But not on purpose."

A setter squeezed between them, barking and wagging his way toward the jar of dog cookies on the counter. The girl jumped and took a step back. "Maybe I should come back later."

"Miss Wyndham," Garrett said above the din, the irritation clear in his tone. "We have patients waiting."

She'd gone from "Catherine" to "Miss Wyndham." He was still mad at her. She couldn't blame him. She'd turned him down, with virtually no explanation. Twice.

Maybe she could talk to the board sometime this week, or write a letter. Maybe that would be enough to change their minds and get Garrett the money he needed.

And yet, she knew it probably wouldn't be enough. She'd seen the shelter, from inside and outside the cage. Garrett did a great job running it, but he was only one man, and one man could only work so hard, or so long, before he burned out.

He needed her. And she needed him.

How ironic. Because neither one of them wanted to need anyone.

Catherine returned her attention to the girl. "Shouldn't you be in school right now?"

She shrugged. She was likely skipping. Catherine chewed on her lip, considering.

"*Now*, Miss Wyndham," Garrett called.

She bent down eye level. "Listen, I'll make a deal with you. If you go to school and come back at the end of the day, I promise to take you through the shelter. We can look for your cat, or see if she's been here. Okay?"

"Okay." The girl turned toward the door. "School gets out at three. I'll be back right after that." She hesitated. "You'll still be here then? You won't leave?"

A twinge struck in Catherine's chest. Five seconds ago, she'd been planning to walk away and focus on her own problems. It was the way she'd lived her two-hundred-plus years of life — no entanglements, no commitments, no regrets.

Surely, *one* more day wouldn't hurt.

Plus, she could work with the animals some more, spend another day at the cottage, soaking up the idyllic atmosphere.

"Miss Wyndham!" Garrett's bark was louder than the setter's. Catherine waved a hand to tell him she'd be there in a minute. He muttered something about not paying her to be a decoration.

"I'll be here," she said. "I promise." Then she stuck out her hand. "By the way, my name is Catherine. If you need anything when you come back this afternoon, ask that nice lady at the desk."

The child gave Catherine's hand a tentative shake. "I'm Rachel Housen. I'm in the fourth grade."

"Pleased to meet you, Rachel." Catherine gave her a smile. "Now, I better go before Doctor McAllister starts giving me shots instead of the dogs." She gave the girl a wink, then dashed into the exam room.

"Where on Earth have you been?" Garrett said over the Siamese cat on his exam table. Mrs. Dawson, the owner, had settled into the chair across the room and taken out her knitting. The click-clack of the needles served as a staccato rhythm to Garrett's words, half of which he knew Mrs. Dawson couldn't hear. He'd seen her turn off her hearing aid the minute the two setters had started in on each other in the waiting room. "I hired you to help me, not entertain crowds in the lobby."

"A little girl came in who had lost her cat. She was upset." Catherine had already stepped in and, as if reading his mind, began handing him instruments as he worked.

Garrett scowled. "Where are her parents? Let them help her."

Catherine slapped a pair of nail clippers into his hand. "You know, you could be honest for once."

"What do you mean by that?" The Siamese let out a yowl, as if reading his frustration.

Mrs. Dawson looked up from her knitting. "Is Princess all right?"

"She's fine, Mrs. Dawson," Garrett said loudly. "I, ah, clipped a nail a bit too short."

She cocked an ear toward him. "You tipped a pail?"

"No, I clipped her nail too short," he shouted.

She nodded several times. "Watch out for those tails. You dip them and they never look right again."

"Okay, I will!"

Catherine lowered her voice and leaned closer to him. "Stop pretending you're mad at me for helping a little girl when you're really angry because I can't help with the presentation on Saturday night."

He finished clipping one paw and started on another. "I am *not* mad at you."

She raised an eyebrow.

He did his best to ignore her, to keep his frustration on a steady simmer. Two days ago, being mad at the world was what he did best.

Now, it didn't seem to work that way anymore. Not since meeting Catherine. Not since their lunch and the impromptu waltz around the kitchen where he'd found laughter — and his smile — again.

Before the fire, he had laughed. Often. When he'd laughed with Catherine, it had felt like revisiting an old friend. Comfortable. Nice.

She'd brought out something in him, this mysterious woman with no identity. Her magic touch extended beyond the animals. When she was near him, he felt different — more like a man than a veterinarian. It had been so long since anyone had made him feel that way.

Plus she was now wearing jeans — fitted jeans that hugged her legs. Although her skin was covered, he hadn't lost the image of her naked and in his office. *That* particular picture haunted at the edges of his thoughts, day and night.

Make that two things he hadn't done in a long time that he was beginning to realize he missed. Very much.

"I am not mad at you," he said again. *Frustrated as hell, wishing you were there last night so I could have —*

Nip those thoughts right in the bud, Romeo.

She was a drifter. A woman without a past. She had no commitments to anyone or anything. She'd proved that lesson twice in the last twelve hours when she'd walked out with no explanations. The last thing he should think about was a future with her.

"Maybe there's another way I can help," she said, handing him the last shot for Mrs. Dawson's cat. Her fingers lingered in his palm a second longer than necessary. "We can talk about it later."

Garrett looked down at his hands. The jagged landscape of his skin still bore the scars of one stupid, fateful night. Yes, he'd saved them, but he'd lost himself and so much more in the process. He'd given up hope long ago of ever recapturing any of that. And now . . .

He'd let that night rule his life for three years. Far too long.

Maybe Catherine left all the time for the same reason he barked at people. Not because she didn't care but because she was afraid of getting close to anyone.

Maybe . . . they were more alike than different.

He took in a breath, then glanced up and captured her gaze with his own. "How about over dinner?"

"Are you —" She opened her mouth to finish the sentence, then shut it again.

"Asking you on a date? Yes, I am." He took a breath, then turned to face her, no longer hiding, no longer in the shadows of the room. "Will you have dinner with me tonight, Catherine?"

She shook her head. "I'm sorry, Garrett, but —"

Everything inside him, all the pieces that had finally started to soften, hardened again like instant concrete the minute she said *but.* "Don't bother saying no. I understand. Hell, I wouldn't date me, either."

"Garrett, no, it's not that." She laid a hand on his arm, but he shrugged it off.

"Mrs. Dawson, Princess is all ready now." Then he turned away before she could see his eyes and the new scars forming inside.

By the afternoon, they'd managed to get through three dogs, two cats, one ailing iguana, a pregnant possum and a frisky ferret. Garrett worked as if he'd forgotten Catherine was there. He'd bustle around the room, grabbing vials and charts, sometimes bumping into her. Every time he did, he'd mutter an apology, then go back to work.

She told herself this was a good thing. The less contact and conversation, the better. Having relationships with other people was a mistake she couldn't afford. Relationships meant staying in one place, committing to someone else.

Being there when the sun went down.

She'd learned long ago relationships and her were not a good mix, thank-that-witch-very-much.

And yet, standing so close to him for hours and having him act as if she didn't exist as much more than an extra pair of hands bothered her more than she wanted to admit.

She loved this job, loved the animals, and if she was going to spend her last bits of human time here, then she needed to do something to make it up to him and smooth the waters. Simply to repair their friendship, she told herself, not to get back to where they'd left off after their breakfast dance.

"I'm sorry, Garrett," she said, holding a puppy close to her chest. The little beagle had the flexibility of Houdini and had already escaped her grasp once.

"Nothing to be sorry about."

She patted the dog until he quieted, giving her a few minutes of peace.

She reached a hand out to his and waited until he looked up before she spoke again. Lord, his eyes were such a delicious shade of chocolate brown. So many people saw him as a prickly, distant man. Catherine suspected they had never really looked into his eyes. She took a deep breath. With only four days left, being honest wasn't such a big risk. "I *do* want to go out with you. It's . . . well, it's not a good time for me."

"Why would *you* want to go out with me? To pick my brain about veterinary medicine?"

Without thinking, she rubbed her thumb over the back of his hand. The ridges beneath her finger felt soft, like a map of him. "Well, most men can't handle a Doberman like you can," she teased. "You are quite . . . amazing."

It took a second, but his face softened and a smile spread across his features. "I'll warn you, I can't fix a car to save my life."

"I don't drive."

The air between them filled with sweet tension. Anticipation. Garrett leaned forward, across the table, his gaze zeroing in first on hers, then drifting down with slow precision to her mouth, his intentions clear. Her pulse accelerated. She breathed in the scent of his skin, tasting it on the air. Never had she waited for — and wanted — a kiss this much.

The puppy, though, was having none of that. He yipped and yapped and leapt out of Catherine's arms, nails scrambling against the vinyl floor, seeking traction that wasn't there.

"I think we'll have to put this on hold," Garrett said.

She bent over, picked up the puppy and handed him to Garrett. "Yeah," she breathed. "Later."

As he walked by her to the waiting room, he brushed a quick, heated kiss against her neck. "Not too much later," he whispered.

She mumbled an excuse about needing supplies and barreled toward the storeroom. She needed to clear her head. What was she thinking? Flirting with him, letting her emotions show. Every inch of her had been screaming yes when he'd asked her out on a date, but —

There was that stupid curse to deal with. *Yeah, I'd love to go to dinner with you. Can we make it a plate of 9Lives on the terrace?*

Hezabeth had cursed her but good. No man in his right mind would ever love her both as a woman and as a cat. And even if she did find that one rare man in a million, how could she break this little tidbit of news to him?

Garrett entered the room behind her and shut the door. Catherine turned around, to find him watching her.

"I never got a chance to ask you this morning. Why did you take off into the woods yesterday?" he said.

She grabbed some bandages off the shelf. "We have patients to get back to."

"You owe me an explanation."

"Why? Because you bought me lunch?" She started stacking the bandages into a pile, if only to keep her hands busy and her eyes averted from his intense gaze. "I can repay you for that."

"I don't care about the money. I thought

—" He made a face, then ran a hand through his hair, displacing the dark waves. It was the first time she'd seen Garrett out of his carefully placed lines. He looked worried and . . . completely sexy. "I don't understand you. You go back and forth. Like you're interested in me and then you're not. Hot, cold. Lukewarm. Hell, I don't know."

She knew how it must have looked to him. Her running into the woods and seemingly disappearing, after what had been a very nice afternoon.

But what reason could she have given? *Excuse me while I change into a cat for the next twelve hours. Now don't freak out, it happens to me every day. Oh, didn't I mention this curse thing?*

Yeah, that would go over well.

He took a step closer. His hand came up and hovered near her hair, as if he wanted to touch her, but didn't dare. "You asked me a question yesterday. I didn't answer you." He moved a fraction of an inch closer and this time, his hand did brush her hair. The movement was gentle, tender, like the wash of the ocean tide.

She had to remind herself to take a breath. "What question?"

He caught a strand of her hair, slipping

the tress through his fingers like a ribbon. A slow and reverent touch, as if she were the only woman who'd ever existed for him. Their gazes collided. Locking. Connecting. Feeling. Doing all the things she'd told herself never to do.

"You asked me if I knew what lonely was."

She swallowed. "I did."

"Not answering you was rude, don't you think?"

"Depends."

His hand slipped down, cupped her jaw. She leaned into the security of him. How long had it been since she'd felt the touch of another?

"Depends on what?" he asked.

His fingers traced the outline of her face, drifting over her lips, as if he were tasting her. Her mouth dropped open, inhaling woods and man. A low, persistent pulsing started inside her veins, growing in intensity and demanding she move nearer.

To take more. Ask for more.

"Uh, what was the question?" she asked. Her brain had become a muddy, befuddled thing.

"I don't know," he murmured. "I forgot." Then his mouth was on hers and the rumbling turned into a roar, pulsing through every part of her. She heard only her own need for him and before she could second-guess herself, she plunged into his arms.

Their first kiss had been nothing — a feather touch — compared to this one. His mouth demanded and gave, awakening the woman in her with the force of a lion being roused from a long, starving slumber.

Catherine's hands came up and gripped his back, pulling Garrett closer. His mouth didn't just touch hers, it claimed her. In all her years, she had never met a man whose very soul seemed to converge with hers when they touched. It was a feeling so all-consuming, so powerful that she wanted to step away from it and yet pull it closer at the same time.

His tongue swept inside her mouth, inviting hers to dance back, to entice him the way he did her. She responded from some instinct buried deep inside, as if answering a call she'd never heard before.

Catherine cupped his face, then ran her fingers along his neck, up into his hair, touching everything, wanting —

Just wanting. There was no way to quantify the way his kiss made her feel. Her breath came in short, fast bursts, her heart pulsing with need that pounded through her like a drum in her veins.

He groaned and pulled back enough to lay his lips a centimeter away from hers. "Catherine," he murmured against her mouth. "Oh Lord, what are you doing to me?"

"I don't know," she whispered, nearly crying with the intensity of it all. "I honestly don't know."

His hands captured her face. His chocolate gaze teemed with unspent desire. "I have never felt —"

"This much need for someone before," she finished. Had the thought been his? Or hers? She had no idea, and didn't care. All she wanted was more. More of Garrett. More of his touch. More of this man who'd given her a taste of the life she'd thought she'd never have, who made her feel like a real, complete woman.

And much, much more of what they'd just been doing.

She leaned forward, the aggressor now, asking for something she had never known she wanted.

There was a knock at the door. Garrett and Catherine jerked apart like two teenagers caught under the sudden glare of the back porch light.

"Doc? You in there?"

Garrett cleared his throat. "Uh, yeah. Just . . . ah, getting some, ah, supplies." He smiled at Catherine, then gestured to her to stay behind as he left. He exited the storeroom and shut the door.

"Have you seen Catherine?" Dottie asked, peering down the hall, then into the room across from them. "There's a little girl in the lobby who's insistent on seeing her."

"Uh, no, I haven't ah, seen her recently," Garrett lied. "But, I'll let Catherine know."

"I thought I saw her go into the store—" Dottie glanced at the shut door, then at Garrett. "Oh! *Oh.*" A smile came over her face and she put her hands on her hips. "Well, all I can say is it's about time."

"What?"

"You know exactly what I'm talking about. It's about time you came out of that shell you put yourself in. She's the right woman to bring you out of it, too." Dottie gave him a little nod. "Just don't mess up the shelves. I was in the middle of inventory."

Garrett drew himself up. "What are you implying, Miss Wilbur?"

"Don't you dare 'Miss Wilbur' me. You go back in there and find yourself a happy ending, will you?" She pressed a hand to his cheek. "I've never known a man who deserved one more."

Then she was gone, humming a love song to herself and grinning like the Cheshire cat.

Damn, he hated it when she was right.

When he reentered the storeroom, though, he was humming the exact same tune and wondering if he could afford to give Dottie a raise.

Chapter Eight

Dottie's interruption had come at the perfect time. Before she could lose her head, or worse, her heart, Catherine had left the room — and everything unfinished between them hanging in the air.

"Do you think she might be here?" Rachel asked a few minutes later, her heart-shaped face wide with worry.

Catherine bent down near the girl. "Shouldn't you let your parents know where you are?"

Rachel shook her head. "Daddy's at work. He won't miss me till suppertime."

"What about your mom?"

"She lives in another state. Daddy has custody." She didn't elaborate and Catherine got the feeling that a lot of hurt and disappointment lurked beneath her words, like dirt swept under the furniture when company came.

Such adult words from such a young

mouth. They sent Catherine back more than two centuries, to distant parents and a disappointed heart. She'd never been able to change any of that in her own past.

But she could change this girl's frown into a smile. Maybe.

She took Rachel's hand in her own. "Let's go."

Garrett was inside the shelter, filling up food bowls. "I'm Doctor McAllister," he said when Rachel came in. He squatted beside her. "I hear you lost a cat."

"Uh-huh. She's been gone for almost two weeks. She had her kittens and —" Rachel bit her lip. "I tried to take care of her, I really did. But my daddy didn't want the kittens and I had to hide them. And then —"

"One day they were gone?" Garrett asked softly, his voice as gentle as it had been with the animals.

Rachel nodded. "I shoulda watched them better. I tried my hardest, but sometimes I was so busy with my school work and I couldn't get to the shed before dark."

"Cats are pretty resourceful, you know." Garrett laid a bowl of food inside a poodle's cage, ruffling the dog's ears before withdrawing. "A momma cat is the most resourceful of all. She'll do about anything to protect her kittens. I bet she's taking real good care of them."

"But . . . but aren't they here? Didn't you find them?"

Garrett shook his head. "I don't have any kittens in the shelter right now."

"Are you sure? Sometimes they looked real big to me, 'cause I fed them so much. Maybe they just ate a lot and —"

Garrett's gaze softened and he reached out to grasp the little girl's hand, a delicate touch that seemed to put her more at ease. In that instant, Catherine saw a different man than everyone else saw. A kind, tender man.

A man a woman could fall in love with.

That was a very dangerous thought.

"Kittens grow fast, but not quite that fast. Let's take a look anyway. Maybe their momma is here. Okay?"

Rachel nodded, sniffling back a few tears. She put her small hand into Garrett's. He seemed surprised for a moment, but then he rose and, clasping her palm, the two of them walked along the aisles of the shelter. The dogs, located closest to the door, barked and whined.

Garrett glanced over at Catherine, walking on Rachel's other side. His gaze seemed to say, "Help me." She bit back a grin. He'd already run out of conversation. The veterinarian who was so good with a lunging Doberman had been undone by a four-foot-tall girl.

"Do you like dogs, Rachel?" Catherine asked.

She nodded. "My daddy thinks I'm too young to take care of a dog so he won't let me get one. Tina — that's my cat — well, she's not really mine, either. I mean, she doesn't live inside my house. She lives in the shed. But I took real good care of her, like she was my own."

"I bet you did."

A beagle came up to one of the cage doors and started yipping. Rachel stopped to pet the dog's nose and offer it a few kind words. Catherine knelt beside her, her hands reaching into the wire mesh, too, scratching under the dog's chin. "You know, when I was a little girl, I wanted to grow up and have a job working with animals more than anything in the world. I couldn't have a pet, either, so I took care of the ones I found." The beagle cozied up against Catherine's fingers, licking at the tips. "Animals and me, we've always had this bond. It's like we have a way of talking that no one else understands."

Rachel sighed and withdrew her fingers

from the cage. "I'd love to be an animal doctor." She turned to Catherine, her brow furrowed. "But what if no one else wants you to be one?"

"Sometimes, you might have to wait a long time for your dream to come true," Catherine said quietly. "For me, it was a very long wait. But I'm here now, aren't I?"

"I bet the animals like that," Rachel said. "Knowing you and Doctor McAllister will be here every day."

She wouldn't be here every day. She wouldn't even be here next week. Catherine rose and looked around at the shelter and the rooms she had already begun to grow attached to.

She'd broken her own cardinal rule. No attachments. She was as attached as she could get. Already, the thought of leaving caused a huge lump inside her throat and a deep weight of sadness in her gut.

And it wasn't just the shelter and the animals that had captured her heart, she realized. Oh, she was in trouble.

It had been easier to escape the Great Dane than this.

Because this time, only half of her wanted escape.

Rachel slipped her hand into Catherine's again and gave it a little squeeze. "Can we go see the cats now?"

"You betcha."

The three of them walked down the rest of the aisle, like an odd little family. Catherine glanced at Garrett and saw him watching her, his brown gaze now speculative.

She'd said too much back there. Opened doors to her past. He'd be asking questions next, looking for answers she couldn't provide.

Yeah, I'm a cat at night but I'm really a lovable human during the day. Would you mind breaking a centuries-old curse by falling in love with me and my cat self before sundown on Saturday?

Not in a million years. And certainly not in the next few days.

"I think I see her!" Rachel broke out of Catherine's grasp and dashed forward, skidding to a halt in front of the last cage on the right. "Tina! You're here!"

She wiggled her fingers into the cage. The white cat Garrett had dubbed Queenie rubbed against them, purring and licking, greeting an old friend.

"So you belong to her, huh?" Garrett chuckled. "She's sure been missing you." He reached past the girl's head and unlocked the cage, helping Rachel withdraw the cat.

Tina immediately settled into her mistress's arms, snuggling against her with a familiarity that said she'd done it a hundred times before.

"Where are your babies?" Rachel asked, stroking the cat's head. "It's cold out there. We need to find them."

And then Catherine knew. The motherless kittens she'd been tracking two nights ago. Lord, it seemed a million years ago. This was where they belonged, in this girl's arms.

"I didn't see any kittens when I picked this cat up a few days ago," Garrett said out of earshot of Rachel. "I have no idea where they could be. *If* they're still around."

"I think I know where her kittens are," Catherine whispered back. "But you're going to have to trust me. What I have to tell you might sound a little odd."

Rachel had gone home with a promise from Garrett and Catherine that they would do their best to find the kittens. She'd left Tina behind until she could talk to her father and convince him she was old enough for a pet. "If not, you can visit her every day here," Garrett told her. "This office could use a cat to keep Charlie company."

Rachel had given Tina a long hug, resigned to the fact that the shelter was a better home for her cat than a drafty shed. "I'll be back as soon as school gets out tomorrow."

Once she was gone, Garrett pulled Catherine into his office and offered her the seat across from his desk. He hung his lab coat on the hook and tried not to think about how much better it had looked hanging on Catherine. "Okay, so tell me your plan for finding these kittens in a city of two hundred thousand people."

Catherine crossed one leg over the other, then back again. She tapped on the armrest for a second, then stopped and sucked in a breath. "Do you remember a cat getting loose in your office the morning you met me?"

Garrett popped forward in his chair. "How did you know about that?"

"I, ah, saw it." She got to her feet and began to pace the room, touching the furniture but not settling long on any one piece. "That cat can lead us to the kittens."

"I don't see how." Garrett snorted. "Good luck finding her, too. I haven't seen her around here since that morning. I have no idea how she got out of the building, but she did. She even snuck past Charlie. But here's the weird part. Aunt Mabel thought she saw a cat that looked just like that one, trying to get into the cottage." Something about that cat nagged at him, but he couldn't lay a finger on what it was.

Catherine paused at the wingback chair, her back to him. "Do you remember where you found that stray?"

"How do you know she was a stray?"

"Well, if the animal belonged to one of your clients, you'd have been more concerned." She turned and smiled. "Probably put out an all-points bulletin."

He laughed. "You're right."

Catherine began to pace again. He'd never seen her so keyed up before. "What if I told you I think I know where the cat is? And that she can lead us to some kittens that might be the ones Rachel is looking for?"

"I'd say that was a long shot." He got to his feet and came around his desk. "Do you have any idea how big this city is? The chances of finding one cat —"

She stopped pacing and faced him, her gaze clear and direct. "I know exactly where the cat is. Trust me."

"I will, if . . ." He took a step closer to her, now inches away from those gray-green eyes, "you tell me something that opens that door a little bit."

"What door?"

"The one you insist on keeping shut. As if you can keep the world out by keeping everything about yourself in here." He pressed a finger against her chest. The touch was light, the meaning far heavier.

She looked away, then back. "What do you want to know?"

"Who are you?"

"You know who I am. Catherine Wyndham."

"No. That might be your name, but that's not who you are. There's more. You don't fit in around here." He shook his head. "I don't mean that the way it sounds. What I mean is you carry yourself straight, like there's a book on your head. And you eat with such precision, I felt like I was at West Point when we went to lunch. You have a way about you, as if . . ." he paused again, "and this is going to sound crazy, but . . . as if you came from royalty."

Catherine flushed, then ran a hand through her hair, lifting it from her neck. Was he getting too close? Treading on some truth perhaps?

"I told you, my parents were wealthy."

"You said they were what I would *consider* wealthy." His gaze narrowed. "That's not all. You have a slight British lilt to your voice. I can barely hear it most of the time,

169

but every once in a while, it creeps in, like when you say *rather* with the *rah* — instead of the *ra* — sound."

She let out a little laugh and took a half step back. "You've certainly noticed a lot about me."

"I notice everything, Catherine." He reached forward and brushed a lock of hair off her forehead. "Since you came into my life, things have changed for me. Yes, I notice you. Hell, I noticed the trees in the park yesterday. The bloom of the chrysanthemums on the fence at the cottage. The way the sun glistened in your hair. But mostly, it's you I see. It's you I want to listen to, touch, even . . ." he paused for a heartbeat, "taste."

She stepped away, behind the chair, putting four feet of leather and wood frame between them. "We need to focus on finding the kittens. Rachel's really worried."

Every time he got close, she threw up a wall. He knew all about walls and keeping people away. "Why won't you let me in a little? You have to trust someone sometime, Catherine."

"I do trust you."

"Oh yeah? Then tell me about yourself. Start with something simple. Like where you're from or where you grew up or what your birthday is."

"June fourth."

"Of?" he prompted.

"Seventeen —" she cut herself off, paused a second, as if she were calculating in her head. "I'm twenty-five. What do you want, a blood sample?"

It was a simple question. Who wouldn't know what year they were born in? Why couldn't she tell him that? Why had she started off saying *seventeen* — as if she were more than two centuries old?

He rose, taking her hands with his, forcing her to face him. "All I want is a little honesty and openness."

"What about you?"

"What about me?"

"Why won't you talk about this?" She placed a hand against the left side of his face, a gentle touch against the most vicious part of his body.

"It's complicated."

She let out a little laugh. "Seems we're two peas in a closed-up pod, doesn't it?"

"You know what? You're right." Garrett placed his palm against hers on his cheek. "I've shut the world out long enough. Let's take a ride. And while we're driving, I'll tell you what happened to me."

Chapter Nine

Dottie's jaw dropped to the base of her turtleneck. "You're leaving early? You *never* leave early."

"Well, I do now," Garrett said. "Cancel the rest of the day's appointments."

Dottie's gaze went from Garrett to Catherine, then back again. She smiled her best "I told you so" smile and then gave Garrett a nod. "Anything you say, Dr. McAllister. Have a *nice* afternoon." Then she returned to her desk, humming a tune to herself that sounded an awful lot like a love song to Catherine.

A few minutes later, they'd gone to a drive-through for a fast-food lunch and were on their way. Charlie had devoured two cheeseburgers, slobbering the ketchup into the back seat.

Catherine munched fries and watched the city pass outside the passenger side window of Garrett's Buick. "It sure looks different from this perspective," she said.

"What does?"

"The car. The view."

"What do you mean? We haven't ridden in my car before this."

Too late, she realized her mistake. She was getting careless. Maybe Garrett gave off extra pheromones or something because his presence distracted her like a retriever in a barrel of tennis balls. "I, ah, just got it confused with something else," she said quickly. "I took a bus to get here from Amarillo. The ride was a lot bumpier and noisier."

"Texas, huh? Did you have family there?"

She shook her head. "No, not really."

Garrett braked at a stoplight and turned to face her, his left arm draped across the wheel. "Then why Amarillo? Did you like the sound of it?"

"I was looking for something." She looked away, tracing her finger through the vapor in the glass.

He didn't say anything for a few seconds. "Did you find it?"

"No." She let out a breath. "Not here, not there." They reminded her of the words of a children's book she'd once heard a mother reading aloud to her child on a subway in New York City. "I didn't find it anywhere. Not yet. Not exactly, anyway."

"Have you ever been married?"

"Me? No."

The light changed and Garrett started driving again. "Why not?"

The answer required more explanations than she could give him. That half housepet clause put a crimp in the traditional wedded life. Instead of responding to his query, she turned the tables. "Why didn't *you* get married?"

"I know what you're doing. That's cheating, to answer a question with a question. But, I did promise to tell you about me." He paused, let out a breath. "I almost got married once. A few years ago, I was engaged to a woman named Nicole."

"What happened?"

Garrett removed one hand from the steering wheel just long enough to gesture to the left side of his face. "After this, I wasn't such good husband material." He said it as if it were a joke, but Catherine could hear the pain and disappointment in his tone.

"Are you serious? She left you because of —"

"There was more to it than that." He

swallowed. "Before I bought my practice, I used to be a different kind of vet." The Buick's heater sent out a steady humming whoosh of warm air. "A racing and show dog vet."

"Racing dogs?"

"Big bucks dogs — greyhounds. I took care of them — handled the breeding, medical care. There's huge money in that industry. The puppies alone sell for several thousand dollars each, if their parents were winners."

She pivoted toward him. "How did you ever get involved in that? It's so unlike who you are."

"Call it love." The words were coated with sarcasm. "I met Nicole when I was in college. She was gorgeous and witty and everything I thought I wanted in a woman. She introduced me to her father, who owned a greyhound farm in Kansas. It wasn't my dream, but at the time, it sounded great, being with Nicole on her family's farm. I guess I got a little taken in by the whole thing."

"By the money?"

"Yeah, that, too. It was hard not to be. I was twenty-two. A kid from Indiana. It didn't take much to impress me back then." He reached for his coffee in the cup-holder and brought it to his lips. A squirrel darted out in front of the car. Garrett slammed on the brakes and his cup pitched backward, sloshing coffee onto his blue dress shirt. The unharmed squirrel scampered up an elm, leaving Garrett cursing and wet.

"You okay?" Catherine asked.

"Yeah, but I definitely need to change." He plucked the slick material away from his chest. "The cottage is a couple blocks away. We could go to Aunt Mabel's, but she has her bridge club today and if we stop in together —"

Catherine smiled. "She'll be match-making again?"

"Exactly."

After a couple of turns, they pulled up in an alley that ran along the back of Aunt Mabel's property. Garrett parked, then opened Catherine's and Charlie's doors. She followed him down a flower- and shrub-lined path to the cottage. Garrett paused at the door. "I want to apologize for what my aunt did this morning. That was entirely her idea."

"It was nice," she said. "I had a lovely time."

"Me, too." Garrett opened the door, allowing her to walk in first. His cottage, she'd noticed yesterday, was much like him

— masculine and minimal, not given to sentimentality and flowers. An oversized leather recliner sat by the television, flanked by an end table and matching sofa. Across the room was a maple desk topped with a computer. His kitchen table was small, equipped with two wooden chairs. There were a couple of photos on the wall, of his parents, she presumed, and a few of Charlie, but none of himself or of any women.

"Make yourself comfortable and I'll put on some coffee," he said on his way into the kitchen. Charlie scrambled after him, heading for his food bowl. The two cats came in from the bedroom, zoomed past Catherine's feet, and made a beeline for the kitchen.

"I think they all noticed you're home," Catherine said, following the menagerie and Garrett.

"Any time I'm in here, they figure it means food." He chuckled. He leaned over Charlie to scoop some cat food into the dishes, then reached for the container of dog food. The cats tried to scramble under Charlie's big feet to get to their bowl, at the same time the Labrador surged upward, reaching for the container that held his own food.

Charlie stepped on the smaller cat, who let out a yowl and jumped on the counter, knocking over the sugar bowl and sending white crystals scattering like a fine snow shower.

"That's it. Everybody out." Garrett picked up the food bowls and brought them out into the living room. "Eat here and behave yourselves. We have company. You can't go acting like the heathens you are."

Catherine grabbed a sponge out of the sink and began to clean up the sugar, laughing as she did. "It's not such a bad mess."

"They're not normally such bad pets, either." Garrett wrung out a second sponge, then paused beside her. "You know, I just realized something. Today is the first time I've been able to talk about what happened."

"Really?"

He swiped at the sugar, scooping it into a pile. "At first, when it happened, I literally couldn't talk because of my injuries. I was in the hospital for a long time. Then, once the doctors decided I was healed enough to go live a 'normal' life again —" he let out a little snort "— I didn't want to talk about it. Not with Nicole, not with the psychiatrist my doctor prescribed. Not with anyone."

Catherine cleaned her pile of sugar up and dumped it into the trash. "Why?"

Garrett paused. "I'd seen myself in the mirror. That was enough for me."

Her arm was stretched toward the counter, poised to swipe up the last of the scattered crystals. An ordinary female arm right now, but in a few hours, it would become something else. Something half human, half animal. Something she had glimpsed once in a mirror when she'd transformed in a dressing room at a Macy's department store.

She'd seen herself caught between the two worlds, a hideous fur-flesh creature. It had been enough to keep her from ever talking about what lay beneath her own skin.

"I know exactly what you mean," she said quietly.

He took the sponge from her hand and tossed it into the sink. "Do you? Do you understand what my life has been like? Avoiding looking at myself, avoiding other people. Just avoiding."

She swallowed. "Yeah. I understand." *Too well.*

He turned away, busying himself with

righting the sugar bowl. For a moment, he watched the remaining crystals swirl back down into the bottom of the porcelain container.

So many years had been lost for him, she suspected, because he'd let one night rule his every decision. He didn't see what she saw. His only guide for who he was came from the unrealistic reflection provided by a mirror.

Catherine knew him to be so much more. She hadn't forgotten the kind man who'd picked her up off the street and hugged a bedraggled stray cat to his chest as if she were a diamond.

"Tell me, Garrett. Tell me what happened," she said, reaching for him.

He looked down at her hand grasping his, then laid the bowl on the counter and drew in a breath. "Nicole's father and I disagreed about a lot of things, especially the way his trainer worked with the dogs, which I had no control over. The trainer was a brutal man who'd do anything to make those greyhounds run faster. You don't want to know what kind of things he did," Garrett said, the words coming slowly at first, then picking up speed as the story began to pour from him. "Mr. Hammond, the owner, was all about making a profit and a lot of his decisions saved money — but cost in other ways." Garrett's jaw hardened. "The cages he had for the dogs were built a little smaller than normal so he could fit more of them in one space. You wouldn't know it to look at the kennels, unless you were —"

"A vet."

"Exactly. Once a dog was done with a litter, I was supposed to switch her to the cheapest dog food on the market. To Mr. Hammond, everything was about the puppies. Once they were born and weaned, he could care less about the mother. Until he needed her again. And when the puppies were being trained, it was all about keeping them in line and keeping them fast. I argued constantly with them, but no one listened to me. I couldn't bear to see the way they treated those dogs."

"Why did you stay?"

"I was in love." The words came out with a tone of disgust and sarcasm. He turned around and leaned against the counter, crossing his arms over his chest. "Nicole kept saying it wouldn't be for long and soon, we'd move on to our own place. She envisioned me becoming a vet at a track somewhere or working at another, bigger breeding operation. That's what she told me, anyway. What she really wanted was someone who could step into her father's shoes. Nicole was an only child and she didn't have much interest in business. What she *did* have was an interest in me, so her father and she concocted this plan to get me there, hopefully make me fall in love with the place and then convince me to stay and carry on the family dog mill." Garrett let out a chuff of disgust.

"But it didn't work out that way?"

"After the first few weeks, I hated it there. I grew up here." Garrett made a sweeping gesture of the room. "My first job was with Doc West. He used to own this practice. He was the kindest man you'd ever want to meet. Had a real way with animals, too. He taught me everything, from how to bandage a broken leg on a Siamese to how to keep a worried Lab from panicking when her puppies were breech so I could get them delivered."

The clock on the wall ticked away. The coffeepot beeped, announcing the end of the brewing cycle. But neither of them moved.

Catherine came around in front of Garrett, reached up a hand and cupped his scarred cheek. In the waning afternoon light, his face no longer looked as shocking as it had when she first saw him. Over the past few days, Garrett — and his appearance — had softened. She saw only his eyes, those same compassionate eyes that had taken her in that first night and made her feel at home. "How did this happen to you?"

"Mr. Hammond liked to show off the puppies, especially during parties. He'd let a couple of them out of the kennels and let them run around sometimes." Garrett paused and toed at the floor. "One night, there was a party. He brought in his guests to see a set of pups too new to be exposed to a bunch of strangers carrying God knows what germs. We had words — a lot of them — and he fired me."

Charlie came over and laid by Garrett's feet, heaving a sigh as if in sympathy for his master.

"I stormed out of there and went to get Nicole," Garrett continued, no longer pausing, as if now that the story had started, it couldn't be stopped. "I thought she'd come with me. We were supposed to be married at the end of the month and I was sure she and I would be happier on our own, rather than living on her father's tab. But she wouldn't leave. She told me if I walked out that door, it was over between us."

183

"And you walked out anyway?"

"Yeah. She told me she had no intentions of being some 'country bumpkin vet's wife' and locked the door behind me." Garrett gave a short, quick nod. "That told me pretty much everything I needed to know."

Oh, how that would have hurt him. Garrett was the best veterinarian she had ever met. Anywhere he worked, he would have been the same caring, gentle man who loved animals like no one she had ever met. How this Nicole could have failed to see the value of him, Catherine couldn't understand. "I think you're the perfect vet. It doesn't matter where you are or who you work for. What matters is how you treat the animals."

He smiled. "See? You get it. Why is that? I've never met anyone who understood me or what I do quite like you do."

She shrugged. "I guess I've always related better to animals than people."

"Me, too. But sometimes, that can get you into trouble." Garrett heaved himself away from the counter and crossed to the window. He stood, looking through the glass for a long, silent time.

Catherine didn't need to touch him to read his mind and guess what came next.

"You went back to say goodbye to the dogs, didn't you?"

He nodded. "You know me too well."

"And that's when the fire started?"

He leaned his arm against the upper sill and rested his chin on top of his elbow. "Mr. Hammond had stayed behind and got drunk after we argued. Really drunk. He had these stupid cigars he liked to smoke. They cost a ridiculous amount of money and I think half the time he smoked them just to mention the price. He had this huge pile of racing forms and newspapers by the kennels where he kept track of everything that happened in the racing world. He must have dropped one of the cigars on the paper when he was trying to get the puppies back inside their kennel."

Catherine put a hand to her mouth. "Oh, no."

"The place went up pretty fast," Garrett said, his voice almost a whisper. "He didn't have a sprinkler system or anything and although the kennels were concrete, the building itself was wood. I saw the fire as soon as I stepped out of the house after I'd argued with Nicole. Hammond was outside, screaming about all the money he was losing, the bastard." Garrett came away from the window, crossing to the kitchen table. He took a seat, then ran a hand over his face, as if the memories were too visual even now, three years later. "I started to run. And run and run. But I couldn't get there fast enough. I could hear the dogs crying, begging for help."

Catherine knelt beside him, taking both his hands in hers. She wanted to take the pain away, as if she could draw those memories out of him and swallow them whole.

"Oh, God, Catherine, the fire was everywhere. The dogs —" He shook his head.

Always, the empathetic connection had been between herself and other animals. But this time, she felt it with Garrett, too, as if there were something special linking them, too. Something bigger than either one of them.

The sound of his memories rushed through her with a blinding, aching force. She heard his anguish, sensed his screaming, frantic rush at the building. The smell of smoke lingered in her nostrils, clogged at her lungs. The horror was almost more than she could bear.

How he had done it, she had no idea.

"Garrett, I'm sure you did what you could —"

"I can't talk about this anymore." He jerked to his feet, pulling away from her.

"I, I . . . I have to change my shirt."

Garrett left the kitchen in swift, angry strides and crossed to his bedroom, swinging the door shut behind him. The bigger of his two cats, however, followed behind, wanting in. He put both paws on the oak, pressing against it until the rickety door gave way and slipped open just enough for the tabby to sneak into the room.

Catherine shouldn't have looked. She knew he'd shut the door to give himself some privacy while he changed. But her feet brought her closer anyway.

Garrett's back was to her, the only light in the room coming from the window. He'd finished unbuttoning the dress shirt and had slipped it back and off his arms, tossing it into a hamper in the corner. Beneath that, he wore a T-shirt, equally wet from the coffee.

Catherine took two more steps forward. Garrett, still unaware the door was open, raised his arms and pulled the T-shirt up over his head.

The sun streamed in, lighting him perfectly, showing everything. No longer allowing him to hide. For the first time, Catherine saw what Garrett had left unsaid.

The fire must have been brutal. Ridges

of lines ran down Garrett's back, some soft, some still harsh as razors even years after the fact. They twisted like ropes around his skin, marring his torso with vicious strokes. It was a picture of pain, of a horrific recovery, of a sacrifice she could never imagine. Catherine sucked in a whistle of air, then put a hand to her mouth to stop the sound.

Garrett pivoted, his face a cold, hard, unreadable stone. He reached to slam the door shut and Catherine rushed forward, into the room. "No, Garrett."

"Don't look."

"Don't shut me out." The scars that ran down his chest were lighter, less intense, as if something had blocked the fire there. Catherine moved into the room, into his space, and placed a hand against his chest, feeling the soft skin beneath her palm, the absence of hair where once it had been. She splayed her fingers against his skin, pale against pale, the touch at once warm and cool. "This . . . this was where you held them?"

His gaze dropped to the floor, his voice a whisper. "Yes."

"And carried them, one by one, out of that fire?"

"Yes."

"How many did you save?"

He swallowed. "Not enough."

Her right hand joined the left, one against his heartbeat, the other on the opposite side of his chest. Beneath her palm, the steady rhythm of his life pounded. "You're a hero, Garrett."

He looked away, shaking his head. "I've never been a hero."

She cupped his face and forced him to look at her. Tears threatened at the back of her eyes, choking at her voice. "Do you have any idea how many people would have left those dogs there? Wouldn't have given them a second thought? You risked your *life* to save animals that weren't even yours."

"Other people would have —"

"Other people would have left them to die! Believe me. I know what I'm talking about. Most people aren't like you, Garrett. Most people could care less what happens to animals that don't belong to them."

His brown eyes softened, studying her. "Where did you come from?"

"The same place as you." The silly tears wouldn't stay in her eyes anymore. "A place where no one understands what it's like to be different."

"I understand, Catherine." Beneath her palm, his heart beat a steady rhythm. "Let me show you." Then he reached around and pulled her to him, drawing her tightly to his chest.

For Garrett McAllister, the real healing hadn't happened in the hospital. Or in the years of solitude afterwards. Or in any of the nights he'd lain awake, reliving every step of that night and wishing he could undo what had already been done.

It came in the moment Catherine laid her hands on his chest. The years of loathing his appearance, of dreading being alone with another person, of being afraid to touch a woman again and have her recoil as if he were poisoned, dropped away.

She raised her chin and kissed him first, and a thrill of joy reverberated through him. Her hands were on his back, urging him closer, asking for more. Not pausing for a second at the scars beneath her fingers.

His words became nothing more than her name and murmurs of need. He no longer held back any part of himself. He no longer wanted to.

Because he was falling in love with Catherine Wyndham.

Chapter Ten

Catherine had stopped thinking somewhere between the words *I understand* and *show you.* When Garrett's voice had lowered into that sexy, intimate range, she'd lost whatever cognitive abilities she had.

And when he'd kissed her . . .

It was a good twenty minutes before Catherine realized they were standing in his bedroom, being nudged by a Labrador who had an urgent need totally unrelated to their human needs.

She dragged herself away from Garrett. "I think Charlie needs to go out."

"Charlie can wait." Garrett pressed his lips to her throat, leaving a trail from her chin to her neckline.

"Uh, he disagrees," she managed.

He lifted his head long enough to see his Labrador whining and pouncing on the back door handle. "Give me five seconds."

She could still feel the heat of his kisses

on her neck. "Make it two."

He grinned, ran out of the bedroom and to the back door, fumbled with the lock, then flung it open and let Charlie out. It took all of a few seconds, but it was enough time for Catherine to realize how far off track she'd allowed herself to get.

Again.

A calendar hung on his wall, one of those free ones from an insurance company sporting pictures of local landmarks. There, in black and white, Catherine had the reminder she needed to quit letting her libido make the decisions.

Only four days left. Outside, the sun began its descent toward the horizon. The sun didn't care if she wanted to go on kissing Garrett. It ticked along on its regular downward journey, regardless. She had less than an hour of light left.

Garrett returned, swooping her into his arms again. She put a hand on his chest. "I need you to take me to the place where you found that cat."

"Sure. Later." He leaned in to kiss her again. "We have plenty of time."

"No. It has to be now. It's going to be dark soon."

He stepped back and studied her. "Okay, we'll go. But —" he put up a finger and pressed it against her lips "— we'll be finishing *this* later."

Anticipation swirled inside her, muddling her thoughts. It was a good thing Garrett led the way because if Catherine had been in charge, with the state she was in, she might have gotten lost in the yard.

They left the cottage, with travel mugs of fresh coffee in hand. Charlie had come back in from the yard, settled into his dog bed and promptly fell asleep, so Garrett left the dog behind.

Just as well. Catherine didn't need a dog around for what she had planned tonight.

"You never told me why you think this cat is related to the kittens," Garrett said once they were in the car and driving down the road. "Or how you know so much about her."

She took a sip of coffee and waited until the hot liquid had settled in her stomach before answering. "When I was talking to Rachel earlier, I told her I have this . . . link with animals."

Garrett nodded.

"This is going to sound crazy, but . . ." and here, the words lodged in her throat. She knew how Garrett had felt, keeping that night to himself for all those years. *This* was a bit different, though. How to explain it without sounding insane? He could end up banging a right toward Bellevue instead of taking her to the kittens.

He reached out a hand to hers and gave it a squeeze. "Hey, nothing's going to sound crazy coming from you."

Oh yeah? she wanted to say. She had something that would burn his ears off. For now, she'd start small, though. "When I'm touching an animal, I can . . . sort of . . . hear its thoughts."

"Hear its thoughts?"

"Uh-huh."

He slowed to let the car before him take a left, then cocked his head in her direction. "As in voices? Or something else?"

"No, it's not voices really. More a sense of what they're thinking." She let out a breath. "I can't explain it."

"Makes sense." He pressed the accelerator and returned his attention to the road.

"It does?"

"Yeah. I mean, it's not common, but I think if you love animals as much as someone like you does, you build this 'link' with them. Your relationship becomes intuitive. As if you can hear their needs. Sort of like a mother with her baby."

His explanation worked for her. Made

her sound reasonably sane. No need to push things by adding in witches, curses and transforming into a cat when the sun went down. "That's exactly it."

"Are you saying the stray I found the other night somehow communicated to you that she was looking for these kittens?"

Another sip of coffee. This time it tasted dark and bitter. "Uh, yeah."

"She did this . . . when? During her mad dash to escape the other morning?"

"Uh, sort of."

"What does 'sort of' mean?"

"I've seen that stray before." She trailed a finger around the rim of her cup. "Quite often."

Garrett braked at a stoplight and draped his arms across the steering wheel. He paused, chewing over her words for a moment. "I know what this is about."

"You do?"

"Yeah. It doesn't take much to put the pieces together. I'm not an idiot, Catherine."

She sighed and leaned forward, placing her cup into the holder. "No, I didn't think you were."

"That cat is yours, isn't she?"

"M-m-mine?"

"Yeah. It makes sense. You move from

place to place, and you can't really keep a cat. So she lives pretty much on the streets. She didn't escape that morning; you probably let her go. It explains why she was hanging around the cottage last night, too. Now you want to find her and you figure she went back to the place where she was when I picked her up."

Catherine squirmed against the seat. The car was such a confining space for so many lies. She managed to eke out a nod. "You got it right. She's mine. All mine."

"Well, hell, why didn't you say so? I would have helped you find her the first day. You must be worried sick."

"Absolutely." Catherine nodded again. Maybe too vigorously. "She's impossible to find during the day."

"Likes the night, huh?"

"Lives for it."

"Well, I found her right over there." Garrett stopped the car alongside the street and pointed toward an area flanked on either side by tall, severe factory buildings built of brick and concrete. Some simmered with activity; others were quiet now that the day was nearly done. Several were shut up and abandoned.

This clearly wasn't Lawford's best side. The sidewalks buckled and cracked in places, allowing weeds to shove their way through. Trash littered the edges of the empty buildings and collected in the gutters. "It looks so different in the daylight," she said.

"You've been here before?"

"Yes."

"Why didn't you say anything?" Garrett pulled the keys out of the ignition and turned to look at her. "What is it that you aren't telling me? What secret are you keeping, Catherine?"

She shook her head, grasping blindly for the door handle, yanking it up and shoving the door open. She stumbled out of the car and onto the sidewalk. Above her, the sky was darkening into deep orange and red shades.

She heard the driver's side door open and shut, footsteps behind her, then Garrett's voice, soft and deep. "Trust me, Catherine. I won't hurt you."

She closed her eyes and bit her lip. "I wish I could. I've never —" she looked away. "I can't."

"Why?" His voice held a tone both harsh and hurt. He came around to face her. In his eyes, she saw how her refusals had let him down. "I told you everything about me. I opened a door that I've kept locked

and buried for three years."

"This is different."

"How? How is keeping it locked inside you making you happy?"

"I am happy," she said.

"Liar." He grasped her hands with his own, moving closer into her personal space. "If you're so happy," he said quietly, "then kiss me and tell me you don't feel an aching need for more. For a *life*, Catherine."

She swallowed. Opened her mouth to say those words. And couldn't.

His hands traveled up to her face, tipping her chin until her gaze locked on his. "I want more now. You made me want more."

"How? How did *I* do that?"

He smiled. "By being here. By forcing me to open up." His thumb drifted over her lips. "Whether I wanted to or not."

Behind him, she could see the last rays of the sun's brilliance against the backdrop of the brick buildings. Time once again had become her enemy. And also her friend. "I have to go."

He brushed a tendril of hair off her forehead, his touch lingering a moment. "Stop running, Catherine."

Her smile, weak and watery, hurt her

face. "I can't." She broke out of his grasp, took a step away, then turned toward him again. "I'll be back when I find the kittens. Please, don't look for me. I won't be where you think."

"Don't go. Please, Catherine. Stay. Let me help you."

A single tear slipped down her cheek. "Believe me, I wish you could. But this one isn't in your textbooks." Then she left before she became a blubbering, furry mess.

No matter what Catherine Wyndham might have said to him, Garrett knew better. She needed him and he needed her. And he had no intentions of letting her get away again.

For a block, he was able to stay in sight of her without being seen. Whenever she'd turn back, he'd duck into a doorway. Then, beside a closed-up factory at Broward and Seventeenth, he lost track of her. One second, she was there; the next, she was gone.

He checked the alley, behind the Dumpster, around the corner, but didn't see her. He crossed to try one of the factory doors when a high-pitched cry caught his ear. Pivoting, he dashed toward the sound. It had come from the Dumpster. He heard it again, softer this time, almost a moan.

He jerked open the metal lid, sending it crashing against the brick edifice. "Catherine?"

Trash bags. Empty cardboard boxes. Discarded computer parts. No female bodies.

Wild, he started yanking the bags out and tossing them to the ground. "Catherine!"

Something shifted beneath one of the boxes. Garrett shoved the cardboard to the side. A flash of pale gold rushed past him with a yowl. His heart leapt into his throat, his pulse thundering at three times its normal speed.

A cat. It was just a cat.

No, not just any cat. *The* cat. The one he'd found that first night. Of all the animals to find . . .

What were the odds?

"Here, kitty, kitty," he called, bending at the knees and putting out a hand toward the feline. She took a tentative step forward, nosing at his fingers, as if she remembered him and wanted to offer a welcome.

He reached with his left hand to capture her and bring her back to Catherine. But the animal balked, scrambling backward against the concrete. Before he could blink, she was gone.

That cat can lead us to Rachel's kittens, Catherine had said. He didn't see how. Cats were intelligent, to be sure, but not enough to use them as bloodhounds.

The sun had set and the alley was dark, lit only by a single bare bulb at one end. Catherine wasn't here. How she could have gotten past him, he had no idea. Leaving the cat to her own devices, Garrett headed off in the opposite direction. He couldn't leave Catherine out here alone, not in this neighborhood. He'd find her tonight, no matter what it took.

Regrets.

Catherine had lived for more than two centuries doing everything she could to avoid having regrets. And now she had them in spades.

If she could have taken back that look in Garrett's eyes, she would have. If she could have delayed the transformation just a few minutes more so she could have made him understand that it wasn't *him* she was running from, but something beyond her control, she would have. And if she could have remained a woman long enough to taste the promise in his touch —

But no, that would have taken her down the wrong road. She sat back on her haunches on the cold concrete and forced herself to think about the kittens. *They* were her priority, not a man she'd have to learn to live without after Saturday.

Too many days had passed since Catherine had last tracked the kittens and their scent was nothing but a whisper now. She should have known better than to wait this long.

She got up on all fours and began walking. She'd spent enough time lingering here. On any other day, being in cat form would have given her a feeling of confidence and security.

She was happy, damn it.

Even if her paws felt as if they weighed a hundred pounds apiece. Even if her heart had sunk to the bottom of her chest, a stone in her gut. Even if the thought of being alone all night suddenly filled her with dread.

Chapter Eleven

"What on Earth is wrong with you?" Aunt Mabel put a cup of coffee before Garrett, then sat in the opposite chair. At his feet, Charlie let out a half yelp. Probably chasing squirrels in his dreams.

He took a sip, but today, the coffee had lost its taste. Garrett rose, careful not to step on his dog, and crossed to the sink. "What do you mean?"

"It's Friday and you've hardly been home the last couple days or nights. When you *are* here, you can't sit down. You spend all your time looking out that window." Aunt Mabel went to him and laid a hand over his. "What happened with her?"

Garrett let out a gust. "I have no idea. That's the problem. She disappeared again. The last time I saw Catherine was late Tuesday. She was going to look for some kittens a little girl had lost. I haven't seen her since. I've been all over that area, searching for her. I've gone out every night, but . . . nothing."

"Did you call the police?"

"I picked up the phone a dozen times to call. Especially after she didn't come to work, but I know she was determined to find those kittens."

"Surely the police could help. What if something happened to her?"

"I don't know much about her. Besides, she's an adult. The police are just going to tell me to let it go." He laid his hands on either side of the sink and watched the yard as he spoke, wishing he'd see a light in the cottage windows, any sign of life. There'd been none, even though he'd left the door unlocked. "And, calling the cops in might make things worse for her. From what I know, she's had a hard life. Might even be an illegal alien or something because she doesn't have any ID and doesn't exactly have a résumé."

"Garrett, this is like something out of *America's Most Wanted*." His aunt put her hand on his shoulder. "Is it a good idea to be involved with a woman like that?"

He turned, crossing his arms and leaning against the counter. "I know this is going to sound crazy, but I *know* her. Not the traditional kind of know where I could rattle off her favorite color or shoe size, but I know who she is inside. She's a good person and she's had something terrible happen to her."

"Like you." Aunt Mabel's voice was soft.

"Yeah."

"Are you trying to save her because of that," she paused, her blue eyes crinkling at the corners with understanding, "or because you really care about her?"

"It's more than caring, Aunt Mabel." He took in a breath. "I — I'm in love with her."

"You are?"

He nodded. Damn, it felt good to finally say those words. They hung in the air around him like happy balloons. He hadn't felt this way in . . .

He'd *never* felt this way about a woman. With Nicole, it had been more infatuation than love. With Catherine, though, his feelings ran deep, almost as if they were part of his blood.

"I'm in love with her," he said again, and smiled.

"When did this happen?"

"Pretty quick, huh?" He laughed. "It didn't take me long to realize how I felt once she was gone. I already half suspected it the other day. She's different from any woman I've ever known before. She under-stands me in a way no one else has. I don't care what her past is. What's important is what she makes me feel in here." He thumped his chest.

"Then who she is doesn't matter to me, either, because she got you to smile again." Aunt Mabel cupped his cheek. "Any woman who can do that has my vote."

"Glad to hear it." He chuckled. "I wouldn't dare marry a woman you didn't approve of."

"Did you say —" Her gaze widened. "Marry?"

He swallowed, then nodded. "I'm through living on the sidelines. As soon as Catherine returns, I'm going to ask her to be my wife."

"That's wonderful!" She clapped her hands together. Then she put up a finger and turned toward the sewing room. "Now don't move! Let me go get my tape mea-sure."

Exhaustion weighed at Catherine as if she were dragging around one of the Duke of Wellington's cannons. She trudged back to the cottage in the early morning hours of Friday, carrying a basket filled with a blanket and three sleeping furballs. She'd found them, but it hadn't been easy, and it had taken more out of her than she'd expected.

No one was about and she let herself in, surprised the door was unlocked, and grateful she didn't have to come up with a clever way of getting inside. Sunrise had come before she could return to Garrett's home and she doubted she'd be able to fit down the chimney now that she was back to being five-five and a hundred and twenty pounds. She vowed to bring the kittens to Garrett's office first thing in the morning and get them the medical attention they surely needed, not to mention the reunion with their mother. For now, until Garrett was available, she would keep them warm and dry and give them some of Ferdinand and Isabel's food.

The first thing she noticed was the fresh flowers springing from a vase on the kitchen table, warming the room and sending out a soft welcoming scent.

Garrett had been here. Looking for her, she was sure. And putting out little touches to let her know he'd been thinking of her.

Catherine laid the basket on the floor in the living room, careful not to wake the kittens, then crossed into the kitchen and withdrew a rose. She closed her eyes and sniffed at the bud, inhaling the dark fragrance.

When she opened her eyes, a white box caught her gaze. A small card had been attached to the outside, marked with her name. A gift?

How long had it been since someone had given her a gift? She'd started skipping Christmas after the first year. There was no sense in counting her birthday when her age never changed. And all the rest of the holidays — Boxing Day, Valentine's Day, Easter — were all just reminders that she was alone.

Catherine hesitated, then reached for the card and slipped it out of the envelope. "I hope this makes it easier for you to stay. G."

Her fingers trembled when she slipped the red satin ribbon off the box. The top fluttered open, revealing a delicate English Staffordshire china teapot, the fluted edges trimmed in gold. Pale red roses skirted the white china, climbing up either side and circling the lid.

And by its side, two canisters of Earl Grey tea.

"I have a pair of teacups to match the pot, you know."

She wheeled around at the sound of his

voice. Her heart lodged in her throat and her pulse began to hammer in her veins. Prowling the streets at night and sleeping on them during the day, she'd told herself she didn't miss him.

She was a terrible liar.

"Garrett." She had to fight herself not to shout his name or fling her body into his arms.

"I'm glad you came back."

"I didn't mean to be gone so long. I found the kittens." She gestured toward the basket. "They'd wandered pretty far from where I last saw them."

"I don't care about the kittens right now." He took several steps forward, until he was inches away. "All I care about is you. Are you okay?"

"I am now."

He smiled and wrapped his arms around her waist. "That's all I needed to know."

"But don't you want to ask where I've been? Why I took off again?"

"No."

"No?"

"I had a lot of time to think the last couple of days. I decided I don't care what happened in your past. You're not ready to talk about it right now and I can understand that. Keep the door shut if you want.

I'm not going to force it open."

"But —"

"No buts. I'm serious. All I wanted was for you to come back. And you did."

"Oh, Garrett." She closed her eyes, leaned her head on his shoulder. "I only have thirty-six hours left," she whispered, more to herself than him. "I wish it were more."

"What do you mean, thirty-six hours? You have the rest of your life if you want it."

She nodded. She was too exhausted to think straight. "Yeah, you're right."

"Hey, the office is closed on Fridays. What would you like to do today? You've got me all to yourself." He grinned.

She stifled a yawn with her palm. "Honestly, right now, I just want to sleep."

Without another word, he scooped her up into his arms and carried her into his bedroom, laying her on the bed as carefully as a porcelain doll. He tugged off her shoes, covered her with the quilt and pulled down the shades. "You take a nap and I'll check out those kittens. I'll be back."

"Be sure you feed them. They haven't eaten in a while . . ." Her voice drifted off and sleep overpowered her before she could finish the sentence.

When Catherine awoke, bright sunlight edged the shades of the room. She rolled over, stretching against the soft cotton sheets and burying her face in the pillow. As beds went, Garrett's queen size was nothing special. No ornate gold headboard. No brocade canopy over the top. Just an ordinary, plain cotton comfortable bed.

It couldn't have been more perfect.

She swung her legs over the side and got to her feet, padding out to the kitchen. Garrett sat at the table, dangling a string. Three brown-and-white fluffy kittens jumped and tumbled over each other to get at the piece of yarn. "Keeping them busy?"

He laughed. "Actually, I think it's the opposite." He tossed the yarn at the floor. When the kittens dove for it, he rose and crossed to the stove. "Do you want some tea?"

"That would be wonderful. I can make it, though."

"Hey, I'm not completely helpless in the kitchen." Within seconds, he had a kettle on top of a flickering gas burner. He fed the kittens, then poured the water into the new teapot, added the tea and fixed them two cups. "How about we take this outside? It's unseasonably warm today. Probably the last nice day we'll have for months."

When they reached the porch, Garrett didn't sit. He didn't stand, either. He paced from one end to the other, sipping at his tea, then placing the cup on the railing. "Are you cold?" he asked.

"I'm fine."

"Are you sure? I can go in and get you a blanket."

"Really, I'm fine."

"Okay. Good." He pivoted, looking, then finally found his cup and took another sip. "Do you want something to eat?"

"Not yet. I just want to enjoy the view."

"Okay, good."

She laughed and patted the seat next to her. "Maybe you should, too."

He nodded. "Yeah. That's probably a good idea."

"If you say *good* one more time, I'll scream."

"Sorry. I'm a bit keyed up."

Catherine leaned back in the chair, propping her feet against the railing and closing both hands around the delicate cup. "Sit a while then. This place is perfect. Paradise."

He laughed. "In the middle of Indiana? I don't think so."

She let out a contented sigh. "I've been

all over the world. London, Paris, Tuscany, Morocco. I've been in castles and on yachts. Slept on trains and in beds bigger than a boat. But this . . . this is perfect. It's exactly what I always dreamed of."

"Why? What's so special about a cottage in the Midwest?"

"It's just the right size. One bedroom. One bath. And it's got those cute little green shutters, with one that hangs to the side a little like someone forgot a nail." She swept a hand in front of her. "Look at the flowers. They're not all growing in ornamental beds where you'd be afraid to cut a rose because it would mess up the pattern. They're in and out of the fence, wrapping in and around each other like they're good friends. And then there's the fence. It's a white picket, just like the one I always dreamed about."

"That's the cliché, you know. Everyone wants a white picket fence and two-point-five kids."

She wrinkled her brow. "How can you have two-point-five kids?"

He laughed. "It's an expression."

"Well, I don't know about the kids part."

"Why not? You were so wonderful with Rachel. If you're half as good with kids as you are with animals, I bet you'd be a wonderful mother."

She stared into her cup. "I always wanted children, but . . ."

He got to his feet, took the china from her hands and put it down, then pulled her up with him. "But what?"

"But I can't."

He shrugged. "Simple. We'll adopt."

The air stopped moving. Even the birds seemed to pause in their afternoon trills. She blinked several times. "Did you say '*We'll* adopt'?"

He grinned. "Yeah, I did."

She opened her mouth, shut it again. "Adopt wh-what?"

"Two-point-five kids. Or, we could round up and adopt three." He laughed.

Catherine swallowed. "What are you talking about?"

His hands gripped hers, thumbs drifting over her palms. A storm started deep inside her brain, rumbling a warning. She didn't want to hear this.

But then his eyes met hers and her feet refused to move. Dark brown eyes, so soft, so kind, wrapping around her as easily as the porch wrapped around the house.

"I'm talking about you and me. A future for us."

"A future?"

He took a breath. "I want to marry you, Catherine." Then he shook his head. "No, I did that all wrong. Hold on a second." He lowered himself to one knee, released one of her hands and reached into his pocket. He withdrew a small dark blue velvet box, flipped the lid with his thumb and turned it toward her. An exquisite marquis-cut diamond ring snuggled into the pale satin lining. "Will you marry me, Catherine?"

"M-m-marry you?" The words barely made it past the lump forming in her throat.

He rose, flipped over her palm, placed the box inside and closed her fingers over it. It sat there, a velvet stone, waiting for her reply. "I know we only met a few days ago, and this is going to sound really weird, but I feel like I *know* you. We're the same, you and I. We both love animals, we both understand them. And we both have lived our lives disconnected, searching for something more. There's this . . . bond between us. And I want to make it a little more permanent." He laughed. "Okay, very permanent."

She put up both hands to stop him, slow it down. Put a pause on this record. "Whoa, Garrett, this is pretty overwhelming."

"We don't have to get married right away. You can stay here in the cottage, as long as you like. You'll have a place to stay, a job with me, for as long as you can stand me," he said with a grin.

She flipped the box over and over in her hand. "What are you trying to do? Rescue me?"

"No, that's not it at all."

"You can't just step in here like a knight on a white horse and carry me away from everything. It's not that simple." She glanced out at the yard, then back at him. "Maybe I don't even want to be rescued."

He took a step closer to her. "I know what you're doing. I perfected the art. You're trying to push me away because that's easier than dealing with me and the question I just asked you."

"You're wrong."

"No, I'm not. You run away when people get too close. Whatever happened to you has made you into a person who won't allow herself to connect. That's your comfort zone and you're doing whatever you can to protect it."

She shook her head. "No, that's not it at all."

"Oh, yeah? Then tell me the name of your best friend."

"I — I," she looked down at the painted white floorboards. "I don't have one."

"How about three of your closest friends? A couple of relatives you visit often? A past fiancé? Anything. Anyone you've built a solid, long-lasting relationship with."

She shook her head.

"Family? Parents?"

"I went back there once, after —" Catherine began softly. "And they didn't want anything to do with me. I wasn't perfect anymore, so they didn't love me. I stopped having a family that day."

"Oh, Catherine." His voice rang with sympathy. "Not everyone is like that. It's okay to care, to get close to other people."

She whipped her head up to meet his gaze. "I don't do that, Garrett. You don't understand. I'm never in one place long enough."

"And why is that? Why do you have to move on all the time? You don't look like a felon on the run to me." He pressed a palm to her cheek. "Honey, I know what it's like. If I didn't love the animals here so much, I would have left every time somebody stared at my face or asked me one of those stupid questions about how it happened. *It's easier to leave.*"

"I don't have any choice, Garrett." She broke out of his grasp and turned away. "There's more to me than you know."

"Then tell me. Take a risk, for God's sake."

Catherine wheeled around. "I took a risk once and look where it got me." She smacked one of the porch posts. "It *ruined* my life. I'm done taking risks. I can't do it anymore." Her voice choked up, as if weeds had sprung up in her throat, and her eyes stung with unshed tears. "The price is too damned high."

"Then let me pay it with you, Catherine, because —" He took her hand in his, closing around her fingers and the velvet box. "I love you."

I love you.

Three words that suddenly changed everything. Her heart sang, louder than the birds in the trees. A funny lightness grew in her chest as if a tank of helium had been pumped into her lungs.

She'd wandered the Earth for more two centuries, sure there'd never be a man who could love her. And yet, here was this man, ring in hand, offering her the white picket fence *and* the two-point-five kids. It was more than she'd dared to dream for herself.

I love you.

The words she had long ago given up hope of ever hearing. The only words that could break the curse.

But only if Garrett knew the truth. And loved her in spite of it all.

Catherine looked down at the box in her hands, at his grip on her, and then back at the warm, brown eyes that now shone with something much deeper and richer than ever before. *He loves me.*

"You're killing me here," Garrett said with a little laugh. "Silence isn't always golden, you know."

She rubbed her thumb over the soft blue fabric on the box and decided to take one more giant risk. "Before I can give you an answer, I have something to tell you."

"I told you. What happened in your past doesn't matter to me. We're starting fresh from today."

"*This* does matter. More than you know." She gave him a gentle shove into the rocking chair. "You'd better sit down." She paused, bit her lip. "You don't have a heart condition by any chance, do you?"

Chapter Twelve

Garrett had been prepared to hear that Catherine had a bit of a checkered past. That maybe she'd run from an abusive family. Or she'd made a few bad choices with alcohol or something. He'd steeled himself for that over the last few days and decided the woman she was today overrode anything she might have been yesterday.

But when she pushed him into a chair, laid the ring box on the railing and started to speak, he realized his imagination hadn't even come close to getting Catherine's story right.

"It all started with a cat," she said. "The cat belonged to a woman named Hezabeth, who lived in the forest behind the castle where I grew up. One day, I decided to take the cat from her because she, well, she didn't treat it very well."

"Forest? Castle? That's quite the childhood."

She nodded and backed up, perching on the edge of the railing. "I told you my parents were what you might consider wealthy. When you said I came from royalty, you were on the right track." She took a breath. "My parents were the Earl and Countess of Wyndham."

"It's been a while since high school history, but wouldn't that make you Lady Wyndham?" He hadn't known that sort of thing still existed.

"Exactly. The land and titles don't mean anything anymore, though. It's all gone. And proving my identity after all this time would be impossible."

"You're . . . a lady?"

She picked at a piece of flaking paint on the wood. "In that sense of the word, I guess I am."

"No, in every sense you are." He smiled.

She returned his smile with one filled with relief, as if she felt the conversation was going well. "Hezabeth wasn't very happy that I rescued her cat. I told you I used to play in the woods a lot and I was always helping some animal or another. You know, bandaging a broken bird wing or putting a baby squirrel back into its nest. Hezabeth was a nasty woman. She treated her cat horribly, screaming at him

221

and hitting him with a switch. He was her familiar, but you wouldn't know it by the way she abused him."

The word triggered a warning bell in Garrett's mind, but he couldn't quite put a finger on why. "What's a familiar?"

"Basically, her helper. Hezabeth would send the cat out to do her bidding, because he was small and could squeeze into places she couldn't. She was always mad at someone or other in Wyndham and delighted in playing tricks on those she believed had wronged her. Her poor cat did most of her dirty work."

"Must have been a heck of a cat to be that well trained," Garrett said. "And you set him free?"

She nodded. "I used to watch Hezabeth from the woods and I knew she slept during the day. So I snuck into her nasty little hovel one afternoon and unlatched the cat's cage. I tried to get out of her house without waking her but I tripped over a chair and knocked the raven's cage to the floor. He let out a squawk and woke her up. She came tearing out of bed, shrieking at me. I released her cat and he streaked out the door. But I wasn't as lucky."

"What happened?"

"She was angry." Catherine's laugh was

dry and bitter. "That's not even the word for it. She became this wild, whirring harpy, screaming like the world had come to an end. No one had ever dared to cross her before. And she decided to make an example out of me. So she cursed me."

The warning bells in his head got louder, as if the entire Lawford Fire Department had set off the county warning system. "Curse? Oh come on, curses aren't real."

"This one is. Believe me. I've been living with it every day of my life since." Catherine took a breath. "Hezabeth was a witch."

Garrett swallowed. Curses, witches, familiars. This was venturing into *The Twilight Zone* territory. He took a sip of tea, trying not to look like a man who'd just heard the weirdest tale in the world. "As in the kind that hangs out a sign for ten-dollar tarot readings?"

"No, as in the eye of newt, blood of snakes kind." Catherine took a deep breath, squared her shoulders, then locked her gaze with his. "Hezabeth decided that if I loved animals so much, I should . . . become one."

Garrett blinked. Had he heard her right? *"Become one?"*

"During the day, I'm a woman. But

when the sun sets," she took in another, deeper breath, "I . . . I transform into a cat."

He shook his head and rubbed at his ears. "I think my hearing must be going. I thought you just said you turn into a *cat* at night."

"I did. And I do."

Garrett scrambled to his feet, backing up until he'd hit the railing and could go no further. *"What?"*

"I know it sounds crazy," she said, her words coming fast and nearly jumbled, as if she were trying to convince him before he pitched off the porch. "But back when this happened, things like this were possible. Witches had more power and they could curse you. And make it stick."

"What do you mean, 'back when this happened'? What was this, last week?"

She shook her head, then gripped at the railing and swallowed. "I was born in 1779. I'm two hundred and twenty-five years old."

"Wh-wh-what?" The world began to spin around him, colors blurring like a kaleidoscope on speed. "That's impossible!"

"I don't age. For some reason, the curse halts my physical woman age at twenty-five. But this did happen two hundred years ago. I was born at the same time the Revolutionary War started, grew up during the Regency Era. I remember the war with Napoleon, the —"

"No. No. *No.* There's no way."

"I know how it sounds. But it's true."

He pushed off from the railing and took two steps toward her. She looked like an ordinary woman, not a lunatic with an even crazier story. "I am a veterinarian. I have a medical degree in animal care. If there were such a thing as a woman who transformed into a cat when the sun went down, I would know about it."

"I'm not lying to you, Garrett. Don't you remember the cat you found —"

"Catherine, when I said your past didn't matter, I meant a *normal* past. Not one filled with witches and curses and insanity."

Her eyes filled with tears. "Is that what you think? That I'm crazy? That I'm making this up?"

He snatched the ring box off the porch railing and brushed past her. "I guess I didn't know you after all."

She'd gambled and she'd lost. Twice in her life, she'd taken an enormous risk, only to lose ten times as large. Good thing she'd never gone to Vegas.

Garrett had left, storming away from the cottage with the speed of a catapult. Clearly, he didn't want anything to do with her anymore. He'd taken the ring, too, so she knew the marriage offer had been rescinded.

Well, what had she expected? That she'd tell the man she was not only two centuries old but also cursed to spend her nights as a cat and he'd react with an understanding hug and catnip for Christmas?

That only happened in fairy tales.

Catherine picked up her teacup and headed back into the cottage. She had thirty-six hours left as a woman and she intended to spend them as she'd dreamed — in this little cottage with the white picket fence, surrounded by the fantasy life she'd never have.

Ferdinand and Isabel wove in and out of her legs, then headed off to climb on the furniture. The kittens awoke a few minutes later and Catherine took them out into the yard to play. She considered taking them to the shelter to be with Rachel and their mother, but when sunset came and the transformation took place, she figured one more evening wouldn't hurt. She deserved one last selfish night, cuddled with the kittens in the tiny house of her dreams.

But as Friday passed into Saturday, Catherine didn't sleep. She prowled the length of the house, trying not to see Garrett in every nook and cranny. He came by that evening to take Ferdinand and Isabel back up to his aunt's house, but didn't come in, or look for her.

Clearly, it was over.

She had her wish. In another day, she'd be a cat forever. No humans to worry about, no commitments, no relationships. It was the way she'd planned on ending the curse. She'd found the house where she could spend her feline life. Everything was as she'd planned.

She should have been ecstatic.

But when the sun rose the next morning and Catherine's body transformed one last time from cat to woman, happiness was as far away from her as the moon. In the kitchen, she put on the kettle for tea. The telephone hung on the opposite wall, silent and still.

For a second, she itched to pick it up and call someone, as she'd seen hundreds of people do in her lifetime. But who? Garrett had been right. There were no friends, no family. Everyone she'd loved was long dead now, scattered like the four winds. Her life had been solitary and impenetrable; she had never interacted enough with another person to miss him when she moved on.

Until now.

Garrett's jacket hung on the hook by the back door. Catherine slipped her arms into his sleeves, wrapped the dark wool around herself, then curled up into the chair on the front porch.

And realized for the first time how very lonely solitude could be.

He couldn't breathe. Nor could he swallow. He should have let Aunt Mabel fix his tie tonight because clearly, nerves and Windsor knots didn't mix well. Garrett paced outside the reception hall, wearing a path in the new cranberry carpet of the Lawford Country Club.

Inside that room sat his last chance at funding for his shelter. He'd been up half the night, trying to work on a speech that would sway the committee members into voting for his proposal.

And instead hearing only words that would convince his feet to take him back to the cottage and to Catherine.

Her story was completely impossible. He was a doctor of veterinary medicine — he knew how impossible it was. And yet, a tiny part of him wanted to believe her. He'd been so taken in, so wrapped up once again by a woman with a pretty face and a believable lie.

This time, though, his scars wouldn't show. These ones he'd be keeping inside.

Jake exited the double doors of the reception hall. "Hey, Garrett, why aren't you in there eating and drinking on the foundation's tab?"

"I'm not in a partying mood."

"I came out here to tell you that we had a request to move your presentation up a little. We're going to hear the proposals after cocktails, instead of after dinner. So you're up, my friend, in about five minutes."

"Good, I want to get it over with."

"Hey, I've seen you gloomy, but even Eeyore would be jealous of you right now. What happened between you and Catherine?"

"It didn't work out. We're from . . . two different worlds." *That* was an understatement.

"I think you're more alike than you realize. If you give it a chance, I think you'll see that." Jake clapped him on the shoulder. "Good luck in there. I promise not to let them eat you alive . . . or let you eat them." He winked, then went back inside the room.

Catherine stood at the back of the room, clutching the basket and hoping against hope she didn't run out of time. She'd found Jake's phone number on the list by Garrett's phone and made the call early this morning, setting a plan in motion that had about a tinker's damn chance of working out.

She'd gone to Aunt Mabel and borrowed a long teal chiffon dress the seamstress had in her closet, left over from an entry for a sewing contest. After a few alterations, the gown fit her body like a glove and moved with the ease of thistle down. The shoes, also a donation from Aunt Mabel's closet, were a little big, but high enough to add an air of regality to the entire ensemble.

Tonight, she needed all the help she could get, even if it was borrowed.

Garrett stood at the podium, wearing a dark navy suit and crimson tie, looking more handsome and confident than she'd ever seen him. A smile stretched across his face and his hands moved as he spoke, invoking his words with increased passion. "This shelter is vital, not just for homeless animals, but for the entire community. We need to care about the forgotten dogs and cats of this city. If we don't . . . then who will?" He paused. "I hope you'll lend your support to the Lawford Animal Shelter tonight. Thank you for your time."

Applause erupted from the audience. People nodded their heads in support, and a few sent Garrett a thumbs-up. His smile widened and his gaze turned toward the foundation's board members, seated at the table to the right of the podium.

"Mr. McAllister, I think I speak for the entire board when I say that your speech was very powerful," said the first man at the table. Catherine had expected him to voice the first objection. Jake had warned her Adam Housen was the most vehemently opposed member. "But, good speeches don't always mean a wise investment. I don't see the need for expanding your shelter. I think there are other ways of spending our funds. For instance, the Lake Forest Golf Course could use —"

Garrett's face reddened. "Golf course? You think a *golf course* is a better investment for foundation funds than my animal shelter?"

"Well, the course is used by many of the people in this room, whereas your shelter is really only for unwanted animals. I'd be happy to entertain a proposal that paid for more euthanizing. That solves the problem, in my opinion."

"Euthanizing?" Garrett boomed. "That is not the solution! How dare you —"

"May I say something?" Catherine moved forward, the basket in both her arms. All four hundred pairs of eyes in the room swiveled in her direction. She swallowed, then continued on. "I work for Doctor McAllister and would like to add something to his speech."

Housen shot her a glare. "I don't think —"

"I do," Jake interrupted. He grinned at Catherine. She gave him a nod of thanks for helping her put the pieces together when they'd talked earlier. "This is a community board and since she is part of this community, I think it's only fair that we hear what she has to say. Come on up, Miss Wyndham."

She walked down to the podium, laying the basket on the table in front of Housen. She gave him a sweet smile, then turned and gestured to his daughter, Rachel, who was sitting at the table across from the head table. Jake had told her that Housen, as a single father, would be bringing his daughter to the banquet.

"I agree with Mr. Housen," she said. "Speeches aren't always an accurate way to measure an investment. Seeing those dollars in action can make the greatest impact." With a flourish, she reached over and lifted the light blanket off the basket. The three kittens inside began to blink and squirm in the sudden light, mewing and climbing over each other with curiosity.

"You found them!" Rachel cried. She rushed to the basket, picking up two of the kittens at once and hugging them to her face, kissing one, then the other, then cuddling again. "Oh thank you, Catherine! Thank you Doctor McAllister!"

"You're welcome," she said to the girl, giving her a smile before continuing. "These kittens were wandering the streets of Lawford. If they hadn't been taken in to Garrett McAllister's shelter, they would have died. Now they will grow up and be loved dearly." She gestured at Rachel, who was now trying to juggle three kittens in two hands. "We could have a lot more happy endings like this *if* you donate to the Lawford Animal Shelter."

"Put those cats down, Rachel," Housen said under his breath.

His daughter frowned. "But, Daddy . . ."

"You're right, Mr. Housen," Catherine said. "Three is too many for one girl to juggle." And she took one of the kittens and dropped it into Adam Housen's hands.

"But . . . but I don't even know if I like cats," he sputtered. The tiny cat mewed and weaved in and out of his palm. "Miss Wyndham! I —"

"Adam, it won't hurt you to hold the cat," Jake interrupted, leaning in toward the other man. "You *are* a member of a philanthropic group. Try to extend a bit of charity to the little creature in your hands, will you?"

"Daddy, can I keep them?" Rachel had clearly spied her opportunity to ask the big question and did it loud enough for everyone to hear. *"Please?"*

Housen looked from his daughter's pleading face to Garrett and back again. "You don't know the first thing about caring for cats. And neither do I."

"Well, that's where the shelter can help," Garrett said. He had joined Catherine at the podium. He reached down and took her hand, giving it a little squeeze. "Miss Wyndham and I are planning on offering classes to teach children and adults about animal care. Provided we can expand the space, of course."

Housen scowled. "Of course."

"Well, I think it's high time we voted on this proposition," Jake said. "All those in favor —"

A sudden roar of pain tore through Catherine with all the force of a dagger. She released Garrett's hand and stumbled backwards, gasping for air.

No. It's too soon. Not yet, please. I'm not ready.

But the end had come anyway. She could feel the tightening and tingling, the signs that spelled the change.

"Are you all right?" Garrett whispered.

"I have to —" the sentence died in her throat when another spasm stabbed at her abdomen. She pivoted, screwing up her remaining energy and started running for the exit before her worst nightmare came true in front of four hundred people. The too-big shoes slipped on her feet and she kicked them off, picking up the hem of her dress and barreling toward the Exit sign.

"Catherine! Wait!" Garrett yelled.

"Mr. McAllister, we're about to vote on your proposal," Housen said. "If you don't stay, we'll move on to the next item."

Catherine broke through the first door she saw and stumbled into the hall. She spun around, looking for a hiding place. Her chest constricted and throbbed, readying for the event ahead.

She had a minute left, two at the most.

To her left was a door marked Maintenance. She flung it open and staggered inside, collapsing on the floor. She clutched at her stomach, biting back a scream, then forced herself to reach up and turn the lock. Never had the pain been this bad before. She had thought the end would be a pleasant, easy thing. Like easing into a pool.

Instead it was a torturous, agonizing death of one self for the birth of another.

"Catherine! Let me in." Garrett's voice.

"No! You don't want to see me like this." The words scraped past her throat. Soon, she wouldn't be able to talk at all.

She heard a thud, another, and then the door burst open. Garrett. Here to rescue her again.

This time, he was too late.

In the light from the hall, she saw the hair lengthening on her arms and legs. Her body began to shrink, as if it was sucking into itself. Her bones seemed to crack and crumble, condensing into miniature versions. "Get out," she croaked. "Don't look at me."

He crumpled to his knees and pulled her into his arms. "Oh God, Catherine, what's happening to you?"

She reached up her hand, touching his face, skin against skin for one last time. "I love you," she whispered.

And then it was over.

Two seconds ago, Garrett had been holding Catherine in his arms. Now, he held a dress and a cat.

Not just any cat, but the stray he'd picked up that first night. The same stray he'd seen in the alley beside the factory.

"It's impossible," he whispered. But it wasn't. Right before his disbelieving doctor-of-veterinary-medicine eyes in the janitor's closet of the Lawford Country Club, the woman he loved had transformed into a cat. "Catherine?"

The cat rubbed up against him, her gray-green eyes filled with sadness and longing. If it hadn't been for the eyes, he might have had doubts, but he no longer did. Only one woman had eyes such an unusual color.

"Oh, Catherine," he cried, bringing the cat into his arms and holding her to his chest, "I'm so sorry I didn't believe you."

She nudged against him, licking at his

face, as if to comfort him.

Outside the room, he heard Jake calling his name. Undoubtedly, the board wanted to talk to him so they could vote on the shelter. Right now, that no longer mattered. He'd find another way to get the funding. Later.

Nothing was more important in his life than this. Than her.

He settled himself against the wall of the closet and drew Catherine closer into his arms, pressing his face into her fur. Of all the women in the world, this was the one who understood what his life was like, how it felt to be different, to be on the fringes of society. Because she was, too.

How he wished he'd believed her when she'd told him the truth. Maybe he could have done something —

"I don't know what we're going to do now," he whispered to her, "but I do know one thing. I'm not going to let you go."

She began to purr in his arms and snuggled her body against his chest. He stroked her head, the lump in his throat so large it threatened to choke him.

"I'm sorry, Catherine. I'm so, so sorry."

She couldn't respond, even if she wanted to, he realized. There'd be no more conversations. There'd be nothing more than this

— the woman he loved as a house pet.

"This kind of puts a crimp in our marriage plans, doesn't it?" He smiled at her, lifting her chin so his eyes connected with hers. In their depths, he saw Catherine. *His* Catherine was still there, regardless of what had happened to her body. "I don't care what you look like. Woman, cat — it doesn't matter to me. Because I love *you.*"

She let out a mew, then her body twitched, stiffened, and jerked backward. A shriek escaped her and she scrambled out of his arms and onto the floor.

"Catherine?" He reached for her, but she darted back, her breath coming in fast, hard bursts.

She huddled into the corner in a ball.

A ball that seemed to grow. Lengthen. Change.

Four paws became two hands and two feet. Fur receded, fading into pale flesh. The feline face was erased and replaced by the countenance of the Catherine he'd seen minutes earlier.

She was back.

"What — but —" he waved for words he couldn't find.

A smile spread across her face. "You love me," she said. "No matter what."

He nodded. "Yes, I do." Her smile widened and she thrust out her hands. "And that's what it took to break the curse."

"Well, hell, why didn't you tell me that earlier?" He moved forward, drawing her into his arms. She fit perfectly. Much better than she had when she'd been a cat. "We could have avoided a whole series of rabies shots." He grinned at her.

She swatted at his arm. "You'd better kiss me before I start talking about neutering."

"Gladly." He bent his head, brushed teasingly at her lips, then pulled back. "Uh, Catherine? Did you notice something?"

"What?"

He pointed first to the pile of teal fabric to their right, then to her. "You're naked. Again."

"We'll deal with that later." Then she reached for the man she loved and kissed him with two centuries of pent-up passion.

Epilogue

"If we don't get this one out, I think we'll be stuck with two-point-five," Garrett said from his location at the head of the exam table. The new room was larger and better equipped, but there were days when he missed the intimacy of the old offices he'd inherited from Doc West. Especially because they'd allowed him to bump into his wife more often.

"I'm not sure I can do this." Catherine wiped a bead of sweat off her brow. "I've never given birth to kittens before."

"Don't worry. You can do it."

She let out a nervous laugh. "Glad you have such confidence in me."

"You weren't this nervous with Ben. Or Elizabeth."

"It's different with children." She wiped at her forehead again. "Besides, back then, I had a doctor in the room."

He chuckled. The memory of the births

of their two children was still vivid today. Catherine had handled labor and delivery the same way she handled everything, with a lot of strength and a little sass. "What am I, chopped liver? Besides, now we have two doctors in the room." He grinned. "Or did you forget you're officially a vet now?"

They'd hung the new white-and-gold sign last Sunday: McAllister & McAllister Animal Hospital. Beside it, sat the sign that had been erected last year over a new building three times the size of the first one: Lawford Animal Shelter.

Catherine adjusted her lab coat and nodded. "That's true. And that means I can do this."

A knock sounded at the door and Dottie poked her head in. "Adam Housen is out there, pacing the floors like any other nervous daddy. How's Tina coming?"

"The last kitten is almost delivered." Garrett caught Catherine's gaze, then returned his attention to the small white cat. "Hold on, Tina. The last one's coming."

Catherine helped coax the third stubborn little body past the birth canal and out of the cat. He immediately started to mew for food. Tina turned and with an instinct born from nature and nurture, began to bathe her new son.

"That's her last litter," Garrett said. He ran a hand down Tina's weary head. "Now that we've finally talked Housen into spaying her. That man is a hard sell on everything."

"Oh, you can't blame him. Look at how sweet those kittens are. Now he's the shelter's biggest supporter." Catherine tucked Tina and her kittens into a blanket-lined basket and together with Garrett, brought them out to Adam and Rachel Housen.

"Here you go," Garrett said. "Three new additions to the family."

"Any more cats and we're going to have to buy a bigger house," Housen said, peeking into the basket. He gave Rachel a boost so she could see, too. "Cats are adorable though, aren't they?"

Garrett glanced at Catherine, connecting with her gray-green gaze. He drew his wife's hand into both his own, marveling again at how connected he could feel with someone else. The two of them exchanged a private smile, one built on the strong thread that ran between them — some might have called it a connection created by destiny. "Absolutely irresistible."

About the Author

Shirley Jump has been a writer ever since she learned to read. She sold her first article at the age of eleven and from there, became a reporter and finally a freelance writer. However, she always maintained the dream of writing fiction, too. Since then, she has made a full-time career out of writing, dividing her time between articles, nonfiction books and romance. With a husband, two children and a houseful of pets, inspiration abounds in her life, giving her good fodder for writing and a daily workout for her sense of humor.

The employees of Thorndike Press hope you have enjoyed this Large Print book. All our Thorndike and Wheeler Large Print titles are designed for easy reading, and all our books are made to last. Other Thorndike Press Large Print books are available at your library, through selected bookstores, or directly from us.

For information about titles, please call:

(800) 223-1244

or visit our Web site at:

www.gale.com/thorndike
www.gale.com/wheeler

To share your comments, please write:

Publisher
Thorndike Press
295 Kennedy Memorial Drive
Waterville, ME   04901

DEC   2005